William Nelson

History of the Old Dutch Church at Totowa

Paterson, New Jersey, 1755-1827 - Vol. 1

William Nelson

History of the Old Dutch Church at Totowa
Paterson, New Jersey, 1755-1827 - Vol. 1

ISBN/EAN: 9783337301729

Printed in Europe, USA, Canada, Australia, Japan

Cover: Foto ©Andreas Hilbeck / pixelio.de

More available books at **www.hansebooks.com**

HISTORY

of the

OLD DUTCH CHURCH

AT TOTOWA

Paterson   New Jersey

1755--1827

By WILLIAM NELSON

Baptismal Register 1756-1808

PATERSON, N. J.:

PRESS PRINTING AND PUBLISHING COMPANY, 269 ▰▰▰N STREET.

1892.

CONTENTS.

FOREWORDS.

From the lips of the "oldest inhabitant" the writer was wont many years ago to hear much about the Old Dutch Church at Totowa, till in fancy he could picture to himself the quaint square stone building with pyramidal shingle roof, and odd belfry; the box-pews, with doors carefully closed; the queer pulpit perched up at one end, overshadowed by the huge sounding-board; the sturdy Dutch folk who with reverential air listened to the Word as expounded by Dominie Marinus, Dominie Meyer, Dominie Schoonmaker or Dominie Eltinge, and at intermission strolled about the solemn "God's Acre" where reposed their dead who waited the resurrection into Life.

The "oldest inhabitant" is forever passing away. Cornelius Van Winkle, Cornelius H. Post, Ralph Doremus, Mrs. Catharine Doremus, Abraham H. Godwin, Avery Richards, John R. Van Houten, David Bensen, Richard Van Houten and others from whom the writer in former days gleaned their recollections of the Old Church and its founders, have all gone. Soon there will be none left who have worshipped within those walls.

To preserve the accounts obtained directly from those personally familiar with the Old Church has been the aim of the writer, that there should be a permanent memorial of an edifice wherein so much for good was wrought during three quarters of a century. Oral tradition has been supplemented by original documents, hitherto unpublished.

There has been added the Record of Baptisms, in the original Dutch, the only early record of the church known to exist.

The frontispiece is drawn from the description on pages 28–31 and the sketch by Uzal W. Freeman, mentioned on page 33, and which was printed in 1811 (not 1825, as stated in the text).

Much of this History was published by the author in a local newspaper about 1871. It has been re-written and revised, and a large amount of new material since discovered has been incorporated. In its present shape it is hoped that the work may be of some value as a contribution to local history, and serve to perpetuate the memory of that ancient landmark—the OLD DUTCH CHURCH AT TOTOWA.

Christmas-Tide, 1892.

The Old Dutch Church at Totowa.

I. Introductory.

For more than three-quarters of a century the church-going people of the country now included within the limits of the city of Paterson attended divine worship at what is known in our local history as "The Old Dutch Church at Totowa." More than sixty years have passed since the quaint and venerable structure was swept out of existence. In a few more years none will be left who can say they have stood within its walls. Already it is difficult to glean any facts concerning its history from living witnesses. Most of the particulars hereinafter given were obtained years ago from persons who have long since gone to join the "innumerable company" who once worshiped at this old church. To put in permanent and available form some account of the history of this ancient edifice the following pages have been written, as a contribution to the local history of the neighborhood.

While most of our older citizens have heard of the old Totowa church, vague accounts of which are handed down by tradition, accurate, definite information concerning it is not readily obtained. The only church records bearing on its history known to exist are, 1st: the Acquackanonk Church Records—one ponderous folio containing entries from 1724 to 1773, and two smaller manuscript volumes, down to and after 1816; 2d, the Totowa Church Records—one volume containing the Treasurer's accounts from 1795 to 1816, and minutes of Consistory thereafter until 1833; another volume containing min-

utes of the Great Consistory and meetings of the congregation,
in 1816, and 1827 to 1857 ; and a third volume containing a baptismal register, 1756–1809, to which is prefixed a copy of the
call to the first pastor of the church.   The Acquackanonk Records contain a few direct references to the Totowa church, as
hereinafter noted ; again in 1810, in reference to a dispute between a member of the church and the pastor, and in 1816 when
the connection between the two churches was finally dissolved.
The Totowa Records are not connected at all, and give no in-
sight into the workings of the church until 1825 and thereafter.
Hence, we must look elsewhere for much of the information as
to the history of the church for the first three-quarters of a century of its existence.   The more important authorities will be
mentioned as quoted.

The Acquackanonk Church chose its first officers in 1694,
and was located about where the First Reformed church of Passaic now stands—partly, doubtless, because there was something
of a settlement there, and because it was most convenient to the
greater part of the congregation.   During the next thirty years
the population north of Acquackanonk increased to such an extent that a church was organized at the Ponds (1724),* and Totowa, Paterson, Preakness and Pompton Plains were represented in the Acquackanonk Consistory by the Van Gysens, Peters-
es, Vreelands, Van Winkels, Vander Beeks, etc.   In May,
1710, Peter Helmerichse van Houte was elected Deacon, and he
was doubtless the first chosen from Totowa.   In 1716, Joris
(George) Reyersen was elected a Deacon—probably from Pacquanac ; in 1718—Simon van Nes, from Singack, or perhaps
from Pompton Plains ; in 1719—David Hennion, from Upper
Preakness ; in 1720—Roelof Helmerichse van Houte, doubtless from Totowa ; in 1730—Cornelis Doremes, who settled at
Preakness in 1723 ; in 1732—Paulus van der Beek, of Pompton Plains ; in 1734—Dirk van Houte, of Totowa ; in 1737—
Roelof Van Houten, Elder ; in 1738—Thomas Doremes, Deacon ; in 1739—J(acob) V. Houten, Elder ; in 1742—Helmech
R(oelofse) V. Houten, Deacon ; in 1743—Cornelis Hel(mer-
ichse) V. Houten, Elder ; Hel. Piet. V. Houten, Deacon ; in

---

*Now Oakland, Bergen County.

1744—Robbt. v. Houten, Deacon; in 1745—Joh's Reyerszen and John Vincent, Deacons; in 1751—Rinier van Houte, Church Master; in 1753—Dirrick van Houte, Elder, Gerrebrand van Houte, Deacon; in 1755—Johannis Vanhoute, Deacon. These are the names only of the church officers chosen from north of the Passaic river; the van Winkels, Vreelands, Posts and Gerritses chosen from the Boght, Wesel, Slooterdam and vicinity were even more numerous. This indicates the growing importance of the church membership north of Acquackanonk, and the increasing need of regular preaching at some place between Acquackanonk and the Ponds.

II. First Preaching at Totowa. *

* It was the custom of the old Dutch ministers to preach occasionally through the week at hamlets remote from the churches, and it is not unlikely that Dominie Jonannes Van Driessen, pastor at Acquackanonk and Pompton, 1735–48, may have held forth sometimes at or near Totowa, though he says nothing of it in his voluminous personal memoranda in the Acquackanonk Records.

III. Organization of the Totowa Church.

The organization of the Totowa church is undoubtedly due, under God, to the zealous efforts of a pious young man, David Marinus, who, while yet a Theological student ("S. S. Theol. Studiosus") was called (Nov. 12, 1750) to take charge of the churches at Acquackanonk and Pompton. He seems to have been a man of some means, and instead of occupying the parsonage at Acquackanonk during his whole ministry, he bought (July 20, 1754) of Henry Brockholst a tract of one hundred acres lying on Totowa, between the Falls and Hamburgh avenue, or more definitely between the present streets known as Marion street and Red Woods avenue, and extending from the river about 5,700 or 5,800 feet north to between Chamberlin and Chatham avenues, including the present city poor farm. The price was £200 "current lawful money of New York," about $500 of our money to-day.* Tradition says he built a

---

*Bergen County Deeds, Liber E, p. 189; Book A of Bergen County Transcribed Deeds in Passaic County Clerk's office, p. 274.

house and lived on this tract, on the north side of Totowa avenue, near the present Jasper street, about where stands an old stone house formerly occupied by the late Robert Field.   Dec. 2, 1760, he sold this place to Gerrit Van Houte, of Slooterdam, for £400 "current money New York" (about $1,000).*   The transaction was really an exchange, it is said, the Dominie removing to and occupying Van Houte's farm at Slooterdam (where the Van Bussums now are), and Van Houte removing to Totowa and occupying the Dominie's house.   This dwelling was replaced by a subsequent purchaser, Albert Van Saun, by the stone house now standing, near Jasper street, as above mentioned.

To Dominie Marinus's residence on Totowa is doubtless due the organization of the new church, which was effected in about a year after his settlement there.   The location of it was also his work, in all probability, as it was almost within a stone's throw of his dwelling.

In the first volume of the Acquackanonk Church Records are several minutes, setting forth the steps taken to organize the new church.   Following is a translation :

The 12 November 1755 at 3 o'clock in the afternoon the Venerable Consistory of Achquechenonk met.   The meeting was opened with prayer by the President and a letter was delivered which was opened and read containing a request from a part of our Congregation at Totua, wherein they petition the Venerable Consistory to know (1) how much service they shall be allowed in the new church [Kerk]† at Totua (2) whether the Churches [Kerken] namely that at Achquechenonk & that at Totua shall be governed by one or by two Consistories (3) and whether every portion of the Congregation shall contribute money for the services or the Salary shall be paid by each [church] equally.

Whereupon Do. Marinus remarked in the first place that he intended to stand by his Call until the matter should be settled between the Congregation and a conclusion was reached by the majority of the Consistory

*Bergen County Deeds, Liber E, p. 193; Book A of Bergen County Transcribed Deeds in Passaic County Clerk's office, p. 277.

†In Dutch, *Gemeente* or *Kerk* is used indifferently to denote a church or congregation, while the church edifice is always denoted by *Kerk* or *Huis*—or *Huys* in the older writings.   The writer has in the translation just given been careful to denote wherever the word *Kerk* is used, as it might have a bearing on the date of the erection of the church at Totowa.

1

That to the Northern part of our Congregation at Totua (in case the congregation shall approve) the fourth part of the services shall be allowed

2

That the two churches [Kerken] namely that at Achqnechenonk and that at Totua shall be governed by one Consistory

3

That the Salary shall be equally paid with these conditions in case the majority of the Congregation shall approve and on this account it has been provisionally resolved that the Congregation of Achqnechenonk shall be called together by themselves the next Thursday eight days at the old church [by de Oude Kerk] at ten o'clock in the morning and then the meeting was closed with a *Danksegge*.

DAVID MARINUS, Praes:

The 20 November 1755 the above articles were well approved by the majority of the congregation and upon the question when the Church [Kerk] at Totua shall be organized, it was resolved that the Consistory shall first inquire how much Salary the Congregation is willing to raise by voluntary subscriptions, in order to see whether the Congregation can make up such a sum of Money as Do Marinus judges to be reasonable. proper and necessary to have, in case the very successful Do Marinus is willing to perform the said service in the new Church [Kerk].

The Great Consistory and Congregation of Achqnechenonk assembled together the 24 February, 1756 in the Church [Kerk] at Achqnechenonk. The meeting was opened with prayer to God, by the President. First there was read a letter from the Northern part of our Congregation at totua containing a desire that they might have a separate government in their Church [Kerk] and pay their own Salary. Next there was read by the President a reply from our Consistory at Achqnechenonk, wherein they grant the petition of Totua on condition that our Congregation shall approve

Which having been read to the Congregation they after deliberation unanimously approved

1

That those who henceforth incline to belong to the Church [Kerk] at Totua shall hereafter be considered as becoming a church on their own account and have a Separate Government & as a congregation combined with Achqnechenonk shall have a fourth part of the service and shall pay a fourth part of the Salary

2

Permission is given to Do David Marinus to constitute a consistory and to perform a fourth part of his preaching service at that place immediately

3

The Congregation of Achqnechenonk is empowered fill up their Consistory,* depleted by those taken out and it is the order of the Congregation that a New call be made on Do David Marinus in combination with the Venerable Consistories of Totua & Pomptan

4

The sense of the Congregation was proposed by the Undersigned and the above approved by the Congregation.

IV. TOTOWA'S FIRST CALL TO A PASTOR.

The following quaint and interesting document, translated from the Dutch, as originally entered by Dominic Marinus, in the Acquackanonk Church Records, is Totowa's first call to a pastor:

The New Call [*Beroefsbrief*, letter of call] of Do David Marinus as Preacher at Achqnechnonk Totua & Pomptan.

In the name of God!

Inasmuch as the Dutch Reformed church in the till now united Places Achquechenonck & Pomptau in East New Jersey in North America have had the Rev. Do David Marinus as their Pastor [*Herder*, Shepherd] & Teacher, and your Reverence having already fulfilled the office very zealously and piously four years among us with Praiseworthy Edification, it has pleased the Richness of God's goodness to cause your Reverence's service of the churches so to grow and flourish that out of the two aforesaid churches, with the general consent of both, a third church has arisen at Totua, which has laid us under the necessity of making changes, and to that End we elders & Deacons of the now three combined Churches of Achquechuonk Totua & Pomptan on Friday the 23 April in the Year of our Lord 1756 in the church at Achquechnonk assembled and having consulted with his Reverence Do. R. Erickson [pastor at Hackensack] as our consulent [Moderator] and after the invocation of God's Holy name we have finally come to these conclusions:

1.

That your Reverence shall perform the half of the Preaching service at Achquechnonk the fourth at Totua and the fourth at Pomptan.

2.

The Holy days mentioned in your Rev.'s First Call [from Acquackanonk and Pompton, viz.: "Christmas and the day after, New Year's, the day after Paasday, Ascension-day, and the day after Pinxter-day"] shall be observed at those

---

*June 22, 1755, Jacobus Post was elected Elder, and Johannis Vanhoute, Deacon of the Acquackanonk church, for the term of two years. As will be seen hereafter, their names appear, as Elders, signed to the call to Dom. Marinus. April 23, 1756; May 27 following, Gerrit Van wageninge and Jan Van Blerkom were elected Elders of the Acquackanonk Church, to serve as Elder and Deacon respectively, for the unexpired terms of Post and Vanhoute, withdrawn to form the new church.

places where they come nearest the Sunday, except Ascension-day, which shall serve as a turn in that Church in which your Rev: shall celebrate it.

3.

Your Rev: shall preach once on the day of the Lord the whole year through. [No vacations allowed!] Six months at the Longest of the days [i. e., in summer] you shall preach once, and after the morning service you shall catechise in the church: and the other six months of the year you shall catechise when and where you and the Venerable Consistory shall agree, and also at Slotterdam.

4.

Twice a year your Rev. shall make house to house visits (*huysbesoeckinge doen*) in the congregation at Achquechnonk, once a year in the Congregation at Totua and once in the Congregation at Pomptan, so long as your bodily health will permit, and four times a year you shall administer the Lord's Supper in each Church.

5.

Whenever by reason of sickness or absence from home your Rev. shall fail to perform the service at any particular place, it must be performed the next following Sabbath at that place where they were promised, and doing this in the manner we have agreed upon among us. as above mentioned

1. A yearly salary of Hundred and Sixteen* Pounds New Jersey money reckoned at half Proclamation money or otherwise New York current money shall be paid you by the Elders and Deacons who now are and from time to time after us shall be in the service, the just half shall be paid you every half year, that is the Ven. Consistory of Achquechnonk shall to your Rev. pay yearly Fifty-eight Pounds, the Ven. Consistory of Totua twenty-nine Pounds, & the V. Consistory of Pomptan twenty-nine Pounds.

2. And besides this a suitable dwelling which was newly built at the time of Do Henricus Koens at Achquechnonk,† and stands close by the Church; a Barn for Horses and cattle, a Well, a garden and Six acres of ground—all these we will repair and keep in repair, which with all the benefits and profits of the same shall be yours as long as you shall continue our Teacher.

3. But should it happen that one or other of the aforementioned United Congregations should refuse or neglect to fulfill their equal part according to their proportion of the service enjoyed by them, whether in respect to the aforementioned Salary or in respect to the aforesaid Repairs, then the other Church or Churches shall have the perfect right (*volkome reght hebben*) to take the service to themselves of the delinquent congregation provided that they shall then be obligated to fulfill the above mentioned conditions.

And for the performance of all this we pledge ourselves as present Elders and Deacons as shall also do all who after us shall from time to time be

---

*In the copy in the Acquackanonk Church Records it was written "*Hondert en Twent*" but the "*Twent*" was erased and *Sestien* written after.

†Pastor 1726–35. Probably the same house occupied as a parsonage until 1888, on the Dundee drive, at Passaic.

called as Elders and Deacons of our Congregations, and before they are inducted into their office this call must be signed by those Elders and Deacons.

We therefore pray the Lord God then let this our Call prosper and cause it to succeed to the only glory of God's name and to the extension of His Kingdom and to the ingathering (*enwinninge*) and Salvation of many Souls. Amen.

Thus done at Achquechnonk the 23 April 1756, in the presence of me
Reinh't Erichzon as Consulent.

The original, in the Acquackanonk Church Records, has the following names appended, which are not in the copy prefixed to the Totowa Church Baptismal Register:

From Achquechnonk:

 Elders—Johannis Walingse vanwinkele,
    Jeurie pieterse,
    Enoch Vreeland,
    Gerrit van Wageninge.
 Deacons—Johannis Wanshair,
     Elias Vrelant,
     Hartman vrelant,
     Jan van Blerkom.

From Totua:

 Elders—Simeon Van Winckel,
    Jacob van Houte,
    Johannis Reyerse,
    Jacobus Post.
 Deacons—Dierk Van Giesen,
     Helmich Van Houten,
     Johannis van Houten,
     Frans Post.

From Pomptan:

 Elders—Michiel Hertie,
    Guliaem Bertholf,
    Hendrick Bertholf,
    Marthe Van Duyn.
 Deacons—Cornelis Teremis his ᴑ mark,
     Joost Beem,
     Peter Roome,
     Albert Bertholf.

V. Dominie David Marinus.

Who was Dominie Marinus? What was he? Whence came he? How came he to Acquackanonk and Totowa? What was his character? These are questions not easily answered at this late day. Corwin's "Manual of the Reformed Church in America" (edition of 1869) sums up his career thus:

Marinus, David, studied in Pennsylvania, lic. by Coetus, 1752; Acquack-anonk and Pompton Plains, 1752-6, Acquackanonck, Totowa and Pompton Plains, 1756-73, Kakiat 1773-78, suspended; 1780, deposed. Also supplied Fairfield, 1756-73.

Marinus was evidently a native of Holland, who having studied for the ministry in Pennsylvania first connected himself with the German Reformed Synod in that State, and afterwards with the Coetus of the Reformed Dutch church, meeting at New York. This appears from the following extracts from the "Life of Rev. Michael Schlatter, 1716 to 1790," by Rev. H. Harbaugh, A. M., Philadelphia, 1857. Mr. Schlatter labored among the Germans of Pennsylvania and New Jersey. From his Journal these extracts are culled:

On the 28th [October, 1748], two Low Dutch students, who studied in this country, named David Marinus and Jonathan DuBois, inquired of me whether I would assist them in getting permission from the Reverend Christian Synod to present themselves for examination to our Synod. This they desired, that if they should receive a regular call in the church they might then, here in this country, be placed in a position to accept of it. I promised to fulfil their wishes.*

On the 20th of October [1749], Rev. Reiger opened our Synod, again assembled [at Mr. Schlatter's house, Philadelphia]. * * * This Synod consisted of five ministers, besides the two Low Dutch students before referred to and sixteen elders.†

Mr. Schlatter having gone to Holland in 1751 and reported the condition of the Reformed church in America to the Synod of North Holland, that body referred the matter to a Committee, in August, 1751, who reported among other things, that "the two Low Dutch students, David Marinus, and Jonathan Du Bois," "ought to be confirmed in the ministry, after previous examination."‡ This recommendation was subsequently acted upon, as may be seen by the published "Minutes of the General Synod," N. Y., 1859. In the *Journal of the Cœtus*, held at New York, Sept. 19, 1752, we find, p. LXXII, this entry:

*Life of Schlatter, p. 186.
†Ibid., p. 192.
‡Ibid, p. 229.

The President read to the Assembly a letter from Philadelphia, laid upon the table by Dom. Ritzema (of New York), which had been written by Dom. Schlatter in the name of the Pennsylvania Cœtus, containing a statement by the Synod of South and North Holland, respecting the two students, Marinus and Du Bois, with an inquiry from the Cœtus of Pennsylvania as to the way in which they should act, since Marinus belonged under our Cœtus. After deliberation, the question was found to be, whether Mr. Marinus should be examined by our Cœtus, or by that of Pennsylvania. This question was taken *ad referendum.*

The same afternoon Garret Van Wagenen, Elder from Acquackanonk, appeared in the Cœtus, doubtless to sustain and encourage his young pastor. For it must be recollected (as shown by the date appended to his first call) that Marinus had been called Nov. 12, 1750, while still a student of Theology, to take charge of the churches at Acquackanonk and Pompton. Corwin, Dewitt and other writers make the date 1752. But the date appended to the call of Acquackanonk and Pompton is Nov. 12, 1750, beyond all question, and the writing is Dom. Marinus's own; yet he begins his Baptismal Register Nov. 12, 1752. On the other hand, again, the baptism of a child of his, named David, is recorded (in a crude chirography, that of the Voorleser, doubtless, by whom the records were kept, 1748–52) in the Acquackanonk Records, Nov. 16, 1751; and, too, Marinus himself records eight marriages performed by him during 1751 and 1752 (beginning Oct. 11, 1751), prior to Nov. 12 of the latter year. The date, 1752, is doubtless generally given as the year of his settlement, because that was the date of his ordination, and perhaps for the same reason the three churches, in making out their "new call," in 1756, speak of the "four years'" service of "the Rev." David Marinus, he having been entitled to that prefix only that length of time.

Wednesday morning, Sept. 20, 1752, the Cœtus Journal states:

David Marinus laid upon the table two letters from Dom. Schlatter, touching his examination, which being closely examined by the Cœtus, confirmed them in their view that the aforesaid student, being under the Cœtus of New York, should be examined by them; and they so decided. Whereon, D. Marinus requested the examination, and presented his documents and testimonials, which being investigated, were all found to be to his praise, and his request was granted. The President and Clerk being occupied with weighty matters, Doms. Ritzema and Frelinghuysen were appointed to conduct the exercise, and they appointed the candidate a text and a portion in the languages. *

The next morning—

The *Examinatores*, proceeding to the examination of the candidate, David Marinus, called to Acquackanonk, first required him to ascend the pulpit and preach from 1 Cor. xii, 3. He was then examined in Hebrew and Greek and in Divinity, in which he gave so much satisfaction that the Assembly found no difficulty in admitting him to the office of the ministry, and whatever belongs thereto. Thereupon he signed the Formulas of Unity, and Dom. Goetschius [of Hackensack and Schraalenburgh] was appointed to ordain him in his holy office, with Dom. Curtenius [of Hackensack] in the laying on of hands.

The Cœtus of New York now write to the Cœtus of Philadelphia :

We must highly approve your zeal for the maintenance of peace and love, shown in the letter of Dom. Schlatter, containing an extract from the resolution of the Synod of North and South Holland, concerning the examination of Mr. David Marinus, together with a proposal to us whether we would find it agreeable to carry out the Synodical resolution.

Our brotherly reply is, that after mature deliberation and a careful inspection of your letter and that of Dom. Schlatter to Marinus, that since this gentleman, with his congregation, belongs under the Cœtus of New York, he ought to be examined by the same. Having thus concluded, we, at the request of Marinus, examined him by two *Examinatores*, in the truths of theology, the languages, etc., and were so satisfied as to admit him to the office of the ministry, and he will be ordained at an early day. Thus you will be saved the trouble.†

The Cœtus, it should be understood, was a body of churches in America formed in 1747 for mutual advice and aid, which finally, in 1754, organized into a Classis and began regularly to ordain persons for the ministry—a power previously reserved exclusively to the church in Holland, and the exercise of which in America was opposed by a large portion of the church here, and hence the formation of the Conferentie to adhere to the old way. The Cœtus was the means of establishing the independence of the American Reformed Dutch church, and founded Queen's, now Rutgers, College for the education of the ministry

*Journal of Cœtus, p. LXXIII.

†He was ordained October 8, 1752, N. S. A detailed account of the examination as above, the ordination, etc., is recorded by Dominie Marinus in the Acquackanonk Church Records, Vol. I, pp. 633-4.

at home. Dominie Marinus was the first person ordained to the ministry by the Cœtus, and the act excited great hostility on the part of the Conferentie.

Marinus married Anna Du Bois, not unlikely a sister of his fellow student, Jonathan Du Bois. They had a son, David, baptized November 16, 1751, in the Acquackanonk church, as stated above. The sponsors of the infant David were Casparus Zabriskie and Katryntje Van Wagene (his wife).* Dec. 4, 1753, Johannis Marinus is born, Johannis Wanshair and Christina Wanshair standing sponsors at the baptism. May 3, 1756, Ezekiel Marinus; Waling Van Winkel and Jannitje Van Houte, sponsors. Oct. 7, 1758, Margarita Marinus; Gerrit Van Wagening and Sarah Van Winkel, sponsors. Dec. 10, 1761, Gerret Wynkoop Marinus; Petrus Poulusse and Annatje Kip, sponsors. Some of Marinus's descendants still live near the Big Rock, Bergen county; Garret Marinus, who lived for many years in Hamburgh avenue, near Union avenue, was a great-grandson of the old Dominie.

Dom. Marinus seems to have been a man of uncommon ability. His examination was a splendid success. But there is reason to fear that he was like too many other brilliant young men— he lacked stability of character and that steadfastness of purpose so necessary to his or any other calling, and to retain the affections and esteem of the old Dutch people, who prized those qualities most highly. All his successes appear to have been accomplished during the first five or six years of his ministry. In 1753-'55 nineteen persons were received into the Acquacka-nonk church on profession of their faith, his wife being one of them. Then the record ceases. In 1755 and 1756, under his ministry, fourteen or fifteen were added each year to the Pompton church. In 1753 he published "A Letter to the Independent Reflector," a small quarto pamphlet of thirty-one pages, reviewing the religious tendencies of certain articles in that paper, which was then edited by the young William Livingston, afterwards New Jersey's "War Governor" during the Revolu-

---

*The entry in the Church Record is in this form:

[Parents]		[Sponsors]		[Child]	[Born]	[Baptized]
David	Annatie	kaspares	Katrynte	David	....	16 Novem.
Marinus	de booys	Zabrieski	Van Wagene			

tion. In 1755 the Dominie published another small pamphlet, "A Remark on the Disputes and Contentions in this Province," under the name "David Marin Ben Jesse, Pastor at Aquenonka." From this Hebrew *nom de plume* it may be inferred that he was the son of Jesse Marin or Marion. Both pamphlets are to be found in the New Jersey Historical Society Library, and both display no little ability on the part of the writer.* But as we have said he seems to have lacked stability of character. After 1761, he resigns to another (from the feminine chirography perhaps his wife) the keeping of the baptismal register, and after 1767 he ceases to keep a marriage record. Unfortunately for him, he lived in troublous times—the conflict between the Cœtus and the Conferentie waged fiercely, and his Pompton congregation being divided, the Conferentie wing got possession of the church and shut him out, so that his friends had to build a new church for him, which they did about 1760, on the Plains. In those days, too, "total abstinence" was unknown, and though it was considered unseemly for a clergyman to get tipsy, it was quite "the thing" for him to stop in the tavern and take a glass of grog; and even the good old Dominie Schoonmaker, more than half a century later, was always in the habit of taking a glass of hot toddy on winter mornings before going into church to preach.

. Marinus appears for many years to have regularly attended the General Synod, or Cœtus, as in 1753, 1754 (when he was appointed on an important committee with Doms. Erichzon and Curtenius). 1760 (when he was Clerk pro tem. of the Cœtus), 1764, 1771 (at the general convention of ministers and elders, which preceded the organization of the General Synod), and 1772. The next reference to him in the Minutes of Synod occurs at the session of October, 1779, when the Particular Synod of Hackensack present a long report to the effect that "Dom. Marinus, then pastor at Kekkieth (Kakiat, now West New Hempstead, N. Y.), had again, at various occasions, indulged in his former sin of drunkenness, and other gross improprieties inconsistent with the holy office of a minister of the

---

*A further account of these pamphlets will be found in the Appendix.

Gospel;" that the consistory had arrested him from the discharge of the ministry, but he bound himself by a written agreement to amend and was allowed to preach again, but fell once more, and was then peremptorily enjoined from preaching. "On this occasion it was also stated that from all places where Dom. Marinus is conversant, exceedingly evil reports go forth of his disgraceful and scandalous conduct, and that he is also guilty of intruding into various congregations, and preaching the Word of God in taverns and private houses." Sept. 15th, 1778, the Particular Synod called up the erring pastor, when he confessed the truth of the charges, but also "brought various testimonies before the Rev. Body, in which it was declared, that for some months he had conducted himself soberly and correctly." However the Synod suspended him. April 27th, 1779, it was reported that he had represented that the Synod had cleared him, and he was still preaching at Newfoundland and elsewhere, and had resumed his dissipated habits. The General Synod, therefore, October, 1779, on the strength of these reports suspended Marinus, and at the session a year later, it appearing that he persisted in his evil courses, formally deposed him from the ministry.* Truly a dark close to a life begun so brilliantly thirty years before. It is said that in these latter days the fallen man, conscious of error, would frequently exclaim at the close of an impassioned outburst of his old eloquence, *Doet gij als Ik zegge, niet als Ik doe*—"Do as I tell you, and not as I do:" Dom. Marinus left the Acquackanonk, Totowa and Pompton churches and went to Kakiat in 1773. The cause of his removal hence is not known.

VI. THE FIRST CONSISTORY.

The list of the first Elders and Deacons of the old Totowa church has been given above, but these men merit something more than a passing notice.

Simeon Van Winckel, Elder, was a son of Simon Jacobse (Van Winkel), one of the original Acquackanonk Patentees. He lived in what was known as *De Witte Huijs*—the "White House," on the bank of the Passaic river, at the foot of Willis

---

*Minutes of General Synod, Vol. I., 72-75, 76, 81.

street, where there was anciently a ford. He carried on the tanning business there. He died in 1775. He was an uncle of Simeon Van Winkle of the Boght and of Wagraw, who was the grandfather of the late Cornelius Van Winkle of Ellison street, Paterson.

Jacob van Houte was probably of Slooterdam, son of Roelof Cornelis Van Houte and Jannetje Spier, born Oct. 26, 1721, and was the father of Gerrebrant Van Houten, grandfather of the late Judge Gerrebrant Van Houten of Water street, Paterson.

Johannes Reyerse was doubtless of the Goffle, and brother of Marten Ryerson, a liberal friend of the new church. He married Marietje Wessels, and was the father of Evert and Marten, twins, born July 26, 1753, Marten Ryerson standing sponsor at the baptism.

Jacobus Post built what has since been known as Zabriskie's mill, on the Bergen County side of the Passaic river, at the outlet of Saddle river. He was a man of more than ordinary education for his day. He removed with his family to Orange county, N. Y., where his descendants thrive and multiply at Postville,* near Warwick. He probably removed thither about 1770–80.

Dierck Van Giesen, Deacon, lived in an old stone house still (1888) standing on Totowa avenue, near Ryerson avenue. He was a leading man in the church, and several times represented it at the General Synods.

Helmich Van Houten was probably a brother of Gerrebrand, grandfather of the late Judge G. Van Houten. He lived where the late Richard Benson lived on Totowa avenue, near the Lincoln bridge.

Johannis van Houte probably lived near the little schoolhouse where the road turns off from Totowa to Singack. He was a son of Roelof, one of the earliest settlers thereabout.

Frans Post was either a son of Jacobus Post, above men-

---

*Now Edenville. "It was formerly called Postville, out of respect for Col. Jacobus Post, whose father first settled the location and owned the lands upon which the village stands."—*History of Orange County*, by Saml. W. Eager, Newburgh, 1846-7. P. 430.

tioned, or else belonged further down the river, toward Slooter-dam.

VII. The Deed for the Old Church Site.

The next document we have, throwing light on the old church's history, is the subjoined deed, the quaintness of which merits its publication in full. The original deed is still in excellent preservation, being backed with linen for greater durability. It may be well to state that the Henry Brockholst who conveys the property, was the son of Major Anthony Brockholst, who did good service against the French and Indians at Canada in the seventeenth century, but failing promptly to acknowledge allegiance to the truculent Gov. Leisler in New York, on the accession of William and Mary to the British crown, was obliged to flee that Province in 1689, with nearly all the other best men of the city. He and Arent Schuyler bought, Nov. 11th, 1695, 5500 acres of land, in New Jersey, one tract of which (2750 acres) was called the "Lower Pacquanac Patent," extending from the Passaic river near the Falls to the Pompton river, and embracing a large part of Totowa. Brockholst lived at Pompton, about where the late Maj. Wm. W. Colfax lived. Henry Brockholst was born December 28, 1684, so that he was well on toward fourscore at the time he gave the deed for the church-site.*

Following is the deed to the Totowa church :

To all Christian people to whom these presents shall come, Henry Brock-holst Esq. sendeth greeting : know ye that I Henry Brockholst son and heir at law of Anthony Brockholst deceased in the county of Bergen in the province of New Jersey out of the good will I owe and the regard I have for the progress of the Christian Religion and especially the Manner of worship of the low duch Reformed Church of holland according as the same is Established by the National Synod held at Dordrecht in the year of our Lord one thousand six hundred and eighteen and nineteen for the promoting of Christian Religion according to the principles and Church Discipline there established for the constitution of christian government we enjoy which prompting for and in consideration of four places or pats [plats?] in the pue of the church now erected and built upon the premises hereby granted and known by the distinction of No. 1 upon a certain mapp or draught made of the

---

*For notices of Henry Brockholst see N. Y. Genealogical and Biographical Record, IX., 110, 188.

several pues in said church freely and clearly giveing and allowing unto me my heirs and assignees forever have given granted bargained aliened Enfeoffed released Conveyed and Confirmed and by these presents Do give grant bargain sell alien Convey and confirm unto Cornelius Kip Robert Vanhouten Cornelis Westervelt Johannis Van Blarcom and Cornelis Gerretse Trustees of the Low dutch reformed Congregation of Totua and to their successors that shall from time to time forever hereafter by the Congregation aforesaid be Chosen a Certain lott of land situate lying and being in the county of Bergen in Eastern Division of the province of New Jersey near the bridge erected over Passaic river at totua* where said church is now built on Beginning Eighty links distant upon a North forty three degrees West course from where a little Brook or run of Water emties itself into Passaick river; running from thence south fifty five degrees west four Chains and forty five links to a stake thence south eighty four degrees and a half East one Chain and twenty seven links to a white wood tree thence North twenty seven degrees and a half East five Chains and five links to a white Wood saplin thence south forty three degrees East three chains and a half to the beginning containing one acre To have and to hold all the above granted and bargained premises with all manner of appurtenances and priviledges to the same in any manner or ways belonging reserving and excepting all mines and minerals unto the aforesaid trustees and their Successors aforesaid to their only sole use and proper behoof to the Members of the said low Dutch reformed Congregation who profess the principals of Religion and Church Government or Discipline Established at Dordrecht as aforesaid to the last survivors of the same forever and I the said Hennery Brockholst do for myself my heirs executors and administrators covenant promise grant and agree to and with the said trustees aforesaid and their successors as aforesaid forever that before the Ensealing and Delivery of these presents I am the sole true and lawful owner of the above granted and bargained premises and appurtenances and am lawfully seized and Possessed of the same in Mine own and proper right as a good perfect and Absolute Estate of Inheritance and have in myself good right full power and lawful authority to give grant bargain sell alien Convey and Confirm the same thus granted and bargained premises and appurtenances in manner as aforesaid and that the said trustees and their Successors as aforesaid for the use aforesaid shall and may from time to time and at all times forever hereafter lawfully and peaceably and quietly have hold use occupy possess and enjoy the above granted premises and appurtenances free and Clear Freely and Clearly acquitted exonerated and discharged of and from all manner of former gifts grants bargains sales leases Mortgages Leases Dowers Entails jointures executions and all manner encumbrances whatsoever without any let suit truble eviction Ejection or any manner of molestation whatsoever of me the said Hennery Brockholst or any person or persons by from or under me they or any of them.　In witness whereof I have hereunto set my hand and seal this

---

*This bridge crossed the river from the foot of Bank street to where the residence of Mr. Abraham Westervelt now stands, on Water street.

2

fourteenth day of April in the second year of the reign of our Sovereign Lord George the third by grace of god great Britain France and Ireland King defender of the faith Anno Domini one thousand seven hundred and sixty-two.

Signed sealed and
delivered in the presence of
GEORGE RYERSE,   HENRY BROCKHOLST.   [L. S.]
JACOB WIDMOUR.

The deed was acknowledged by Brockholst the same day, before George Ryerse, "one of His Majesty's Judges of the Court of Common Pleas for Bergen county." It was recorded August 20, 1802, in the Bergen County Clerk's office in Book P of Deeds, p. 114, and is in Bergen County Transcribed Deeds, in the Passaic County Clerk's office, Book C, p. 90.

VIII. THE TRUSTEES IN 1762.

A few words may be appropriate concerning the Consistory, mentioned as Trustees in the deed of 1762.

Cornelis Kip was doubtless the co-partner of George De Riemers (Doremus) in the purchase of the Preakness tract, in 1723; and lived at Preakness.

Robert Vanhouten and his wife Elizabeth Post joined the Acquackanonk church in 1738; he was elected Deacon in 1744. He lived west of Totowa, near the Singack road, and was the father of Adrian (born 1750) and Cornelus (born 1753).

Cornelis Westervelt lived near Wagraw, and was the grandfather of the late Cornelius I. Westervelt, for many years President of the Paterson Gas Light Company.

Johannis Van Blerkom lived at the southwest corner of Willis street and Vreeland avenue, in an old stone house destroyed about 1870. He had several children, one of whom, Henry, served creditably in an engagement at Fort Lee, in the Revolution. Johannis was the great-grandfather of the late ex-Mayor Brant Van Blarcom.

Cornelus Gerretse was a large land-owner at the Boght and lived there about the time the deed was given, about where the old Van Winkle homestead (late Riverside Hotel) stood prior to 1873. He sold this property to Simeon Van Winkle, who married his daughter Margaret about 1780. This Simeon was the grandfather of the late Cornelius Van Winkle, who was named after old Cornelus Gerretse or Garrison.

IX. The Church on the Hill-Side.

The plot of land given by Brockholst for a church site was almost triangular in shape, and was intersected by that part of the old Totowa road lying between the present Hamburgh and Totowa avenues, and from 1870 to 1887 called Water street, but now Ryle avenue. The northerly line would run parallel to Matlock street, and about one hundred feet south of that street. The south line of the present quarry road, running westerly from Ryle avenue, if extended northeasterly would be the line of the old plot. The easterly line ran within fifteen or twenty feet of the brook, or seventy-five to one hundred feet west of the present Hamburgh avenue. Thus the better and larger part of the tract lay north of the Totowa road, now Ryle avenue. The property included the lots designated on the city map as No.'s 45 to 56 inclusive, 57 and 59 Water street.

Thus, near the foot of the hill, upon the principal road north of the Passaic, within a stone's throw of the bright and rushing brook which flowed free and unconfined on one hand, and of the rippling Passaic on the other, with the roar of the mighty and undespoiled cataract ever sounding near; convenient to the only bridge which then spanned the Passaic river north of the town of Newark; and also (important consideration) convenient to the inn where "refreshment for man and beast" was kept by Abraham Godwin (father of the old General) in the quaint, low stone house, recently the kitchen and dining room of Mr. Cornelius Benson, in Water street, and torn down only in 1886, but at that time directly opposite the north end of the solitary bridge—here we say, under the shadow of the forest-crowned hill, snugly sheltered from boreal blasts, did these God-fearing people erect their tabernacle for the Lord's worship. And here for nearly three-quarters of a century, did they assemble once or twice a month to hear the Word expounded in solemn and impressive Dutch.

The deed for the church-site speaks of the edifice as already built. Probably Brockholst had promised Dominie Marinus (whose preaching he must have heard at Pompton) to give the land if he should get a church built here. There is every reason to believe that the building had been started, at least, fully seven years before the deed was passed.

The first published notice of the old church is doubtless that of the Marquis de Chastellux, a warm friend of Lafayette's, who traveled with the American army in 1780-2. In his Journal[*] he describes the location of the American Army on Totowa and Manchester Heights :

"It was encamped on two heights, and in one line, in an extended but very good position, having a wood in the rear, and in the front the river, which is very difficult of passage everywhere except at Totohaw-Bridge. * * Two miles beyond the bridge is a meeting-house of an hexagonal form, which is given to their places of worship by the Dutch Presbyterians, who are very numerous in the Jerseys."[†]

Thus de Chastellux. The word "hexagonal" was probably due to a slip in his memory, for in this case, at all events, it was as incorrect as the statement of the distance of the church from the bridge.

The exact location of the old church was about thirty feet east of the Totowa road (now Ryle avenue), about one hundred feet south of Matlock street, or on the rear of Lot No. 45 Water street (as on the present city map) and on the upper part of Lot No. 47.

X. Its External Appearance.

It was about 30x40 feet in area, possibly a little larger. The stone walls were only eighteen or twenty feet high, and the shingled roof overhung them two or three feet, making the walls appear much lower than they really were. The roof rose from all four sides with quite a steep pitch to a common point, which was surmounted by a belfry of great simplicity of construction—four posts like legs straddling over the pyramid-

---

[*]Travels in North America, etc., London, 1787, Vol. I., p. 109.

[†]The original edition reads : "A deux milles au-dela du pont, on trouve un Meeting-House de forme exagone," etc.—*Voyages de M. le Marquis de Chastellux dans L'Amerique Septentrionale dans les annees* 1780, 1781 & 1782. Paris, 1786. I., 95. Had the Marquis inserted the word "pieds" after the word "milles" he would have been less inaccurate, although the church was not even two thousand feet, much less two miles, from the bridge. The distance was less than five hundred feet, indeed.

al apex, supporting a miniature shingle roof, which sheltered
from the storms, in a measure, but left in plain view the bell
and its attendant wheel, by which the people were summoned
to service.   This quaint belfry was capped by a weathercock,
which flaunted his golden plumage in storm and sunshine for
many, many years, his giddy evolutions contrasting strangely
with the steadfastness of purpose of those whose voices on the
Lord's Day ascended up through the not over-close roof be-
neath him.   It must have been a quaint-looking building, altogether, but its plan was very similar to that of all the early
Dutch churches in America.   The doorway in the middle of
the front, towards the Totowa road, was quite spacious, was
fronted by a broad step of brownstone, and flanked on either
side by a large window.   On each side of the building were
two other similar windows, the top of each and all being turned with a brick arch, as was also the top of the door.   There
were no windows in the rear.

It is said that on one stone on the south side wall there was
rudely sculptured a heart in outline, and on another a diamond,
the former inclosing the initials of Marten Ryerson, and the
latter those of his wife Annetje Van Rypen, of whom more
anon.   Hence the following story: One day a blacksmith
down the road saw an Irishman pounding away at the door of
the church.   He hallooed to him, "What do you want, Pat?"
"Sure an' I want a pack of cards."   "Cards! How do you ex-
pect to get cards there? What do you take that building for?"
"Troth an' I thought it was a card factory!"   "A 'card factory!'
Why, man, you must be crazy : what put that notion into your
head?"   "Faith, and didn't I see the ace of hearts an' the ace of
diamonds on the wall, an' I thought them the advertisement of
a card factory."   Pat was mightily taken back when informed
that it was a church.   The Marten Ryerson referred to was a
son of Frans Ryerson, of New York, one of the earliest purchasers of the Wagraw tract.   Marten lived in an old stone
house torn down about 1870-72, near the corner of Clinton
and Water streets, Clinton street being the westerly line of
his property.   They were interred in a private burying-ground
in the rear of the old stone house, No. 117 Water street, whence

the bodies were removed many years later to the old Dutch
cemetery, south of the quarry road. Some years ago a grand-
son, Martin Ryerson, then living in Chicago, had the still
handsome marble box-tombs removed to Cedar Lawn cemetery.
He died in 1787, aged 79 years; his wife, 1784, aged 68
years. One of the daughters of old Marten Ryerson married
James McCurdy, from whom McCurdy's pond took its name.
Tradition differs as to the part Ryerson took in the building of
the old church—some saying that he did the mason work, and
others that he gave largely of his means to help on the under-
taking, and hence the privilege accorded him of perpetuating
his name in the walls of the church.

Over the doorway, in front, was a whitish or light-colored
stone, smoothly cut and polished, about sixteen inches square,
but inserted in the wall so as to present the form of a diamond,
and in this stone was deeply inscribed this inscription :

"This [is] the House of the Lord, 1755."

The late Avery Richards, of Paterson, who lived for many
years in the old frame house still standing (1888) at the northeast corner of Broadway and Carroll street, was the only person the writer ever found who could recollect that date, but
he remembered it very distinctly, from the time he first saw it
in 1819, and his recollection was undoubtedly correct, being
sustained also by collateral evidence *

Mr. Richards, by the way, when a mere lad, heard his
great-uncle, Daniel Fuller, a soldier of the New Hampshire

*In the printed pamphlet of the late Judge Dickerson's Historical Sketch of Pater-
erson he gives this date as 1745—clearly a blunder, and doubtless a misprint for 1755.

Line in the Revolution, and quartered hereabout one or two winters, tell how he and the rest of a foraging party of soldiers "camped" one night in this very church, "close by the Great Falls."

In front of the church stood a majestic oak tree, which threw its grateful shade over all the space between the church and the road, and its long arms reached out lovingly to the quaint building as if it would fain encircle it in its mighty embrace. For sixty or seventy years did that oak wax grander and lustier. Then, for some reason never explained, it was cut down, to the general regret, it seems, of the whole congregation, for the event was considered of such importance that it is remembered *who* laid the axe to that trunk the girt of which was upward of ten feet—it was Cornelius G. Post. It has been suggested that it afforded too convenient a shade for loiterers during service, but the true explanation doubtless is that the Consistory were on some occasion hard pressed for money, and sold the tree to replenish their treasury. But the old people in years after always connected the felling of that tree with the subsequent destruction of the church! On the north side of the building, up the hill, stood a great buttonwood tree, whose rapidly growing branches, with adjacent undergrowth, formed a favorite and sheltered retreat for the women and children of the congregation.

XI. INTERNAL APPEARANCE.

Entering the front door (and there was no other) the congregation were immediately in the audience room of the building, there being no vestibule or ante-room. A narrow stairway on either side ran up to the two galleries. The floor was occupied by two double rows of pews—straight, high-backed affairs, with doors to them, the rows being separated by an aisle stretching up the middle of the church. The pews were quite long. Along against each of the side-walls was a high-backed bench, whereon the boys and youths were accustomed to sit, and in front of them, occupying a similar long bench, running the length of the church, sat the slaves and "free persons of color." Human nature was much the same then as now, it seems, for it is related that the mischievous urchins and youths on the back seats used to "wile away the weary hour" of the Dominie's sermon by carving holes in the backs of the seats before them, and with sundry pins and the like were wont to prod the backs of the aforesaid slaves and free persons of color! But the most striking object that greeted the eye on entering the church was the pulpit. How shall we describe that wonderful product of the carpenter's craft? Fancy a shanghai rooster cut in two vertically and latitudinally, his front half placed up against a wall, and his head cut off and suspended an inch or two above him. Or, it has been described as being like a swallow's nest. Or, like the half of a newel-post cut in two perpendicularly. It was a semi-octagonal box placed against the rear wall, tapering down to a mere post at the floor. This swallow's nest pulpit, only about large enough for one person, was reached by a narrow and steep step-ladder, and the Dominie when mounted to his perch was eight or ten feet above the mass of his congregation, and could almost look down upon the few who occasionally gathered in the galleries. Above him was suspended, like a great umbrella, or like the lid of a box (and we wonder if the preachers who sometimes uttered nonsense in those days did not fear, while talking, that this lid would suddenly come down upon them like an old-fashioned candle-extinguisher?), that wonderful, ancient contrivance known as a sounding-board, which was supposed to catch all the preacher's eloquence and hurl it down upon the congregation below him. This was an elaborate eight-cornered affair, extending from the wall, and supported by a large iron bar which projected several feet out from the wall and held the sounding-board from above. The galleries simply contained long benches, but no pews; the face of the galleries was a kind of open lattice-work, of half-rounded rails—like stair bannisters. The ceiling sloped up like the roof, from the four sides toward a common centre, but in the middle there was a flat space; the whole was ceiled with boards, instead of plastered, and the whole interior was painted a dingy drab. The Elders occupied a pew on the right of the pulpit, and the Deacons sat on the left. Before the pulpit, and about six feet from it, was a little box, with a book-rest rising before it, for the accommodation of the man who, next to the Dominie, was altogether the most essential to the successful holding of service in the church. This was the *Voorleser*—the fore-reader or singer, a position occupied in the old Totowa church for many years, with great acceptance, by Albert Van Saun, father of the late Samuel A. Van Saun.

Thus we have described the exterior and the interior of the old church, as it appeared from 1755 until 1816, when it was overhauled. But, says the reader, "Stop, you have told us nothing about the heating and lighting of the church." True, but there were no appliances of the sort about the building; there was preaching there only every third Sunday, and as the people came long distances night meetings were out of the question. As for the heating, everybody carried his or her foot-stove, or if not, suffered accordingly. But the ladies never forgot in winter their warming-pan or foot-stove—a tin box on a stout wooden frame, filled with live hickory coals, covered with ashes which were raked occasionally as the fire grew dull, the tin perforated with holes to let the heat escape and give the fire ventilation. With such a contrivance as this under their feet the ladies kept far more comfortable, generally, than their successors do in badly-ventilated buildings, where all the cold air settles on the floor to chill people's feet through. In these olden times when one got her feet thoroughly warmed she pushed the foot-stove along to the next, and so on. About 1812 or 1814 box stoves were introduced to warm the church, but the elderly ladies always carried their own stoves with them still.

It is said that there was a sketch or view of the church drawn by old Gen. Abraham Godwin, once upon a time, on the walls of the Passaic Hotel, which was so admirable and striking a likeness that his son declared it should always remain, but it was whitewashed over many years ago. There is a crude sketch of the building still in existence on a map of the adjacent Wallis property, executed by Uzal W. Freeman, a local surveyor, about 1825.

3

XII. Church Going in the Olden Time.

It is a bright Sunday morning say a hundred years ago, and it is the "turn" of the Totowa church people to have service in their *Kerk*—on the Hillside. The Voorleser and sexton stands in the middle aisle of the old church, in the centre of the building, vigorously pulls the rope that dangles down from the bell through the roof nearly to the floor, and the wheel in the belfry gives a whirl and the bell turns and clangs out its call to the people. Along the few roads leading hither great wagons are seen slowly wending their way churchward, while far more numerous are the groups of horsemen and horsewomen, who prefer that means of conveyance to jolting in heavy wagons devoid of springs over the rough roads. As the appointed hour draws nigh the people gather about the church, awaiting the coming of the Dominie. He arrives in good season, and after appropriately greeting his parishioners on every side, he enters the church, followed by the congregation, who with becoming gravity take their accustomed places, paterfamilias closing the door of his pew as the last of his flock enters. On ascending to the pulpit the Dominie kneels, bows his head, holding up his hat before his face, and silently prays, the congregation likewise engaging in silent prayer. Then he announces a hymn to be sung, or (as was the custom in those earlier days) hands the Voorleser a notice of the hymn selected. The Voorleser stands up in his place before the pulpit, and placing his book in a rack before him starts the tune and leads the singing, *all* the congregation joining. And with what fervor, and how sonorously they chorus the praises of Jehovah! There is no violin, nor bass-viol, nor organ to keep the accompaniment, and no choir to do the singing. The congregation feel that everything depends on their voices, and most heartily do they respond. If you want to hear such singing now, attend one of our Holland churches some Sunday. The Dominie now offers up a brief invocation to God, and then announces a chapter in the Bible, which the Voorleser stands up and reads. After this the pastor gives out another hymn, which is sung as before, the Voorleser leading, and then the congregation settle themselves for a good, full hour's discourse, under the several heads of "firstly" to "twenty-firstly." Of course the young people thought this terribly prosy, but the longer and more controversial the discourses were the better the old people enjoyed them, for be it remembered they heard a sermon but every third Sunday, and most of them came miles to hear that. The sermon over, the Deacons arise, grasp the long poles in their pew and sally out among the congregation to take up the usual collection—originally sacredly devoted to establishing a fund for the payment of the pastor's salary. The poles are six or eight feet long, to reach the end of the long pews, and on the extremity of each pole is attached a small black bag with a little bell at the bottom which answers a double purpose—awaking sleepers (some of the congregation were remarkably drowsy during the ceremony), and announcing by its responsive jingle, whenever any coppers were dropped in. About 1816, the bells were taken off the collection bags, which were retained in use, however, till the burning of the old church. This sort of "contribution box" was common in all Dutch churches during the last century. The Dominie now offers up another short prayer and dismisses the congregation for three weeks. The service lasted from half-past ten o'clock in the morning until one or half-past one in the afternoon. When the Sacrament of the Lord's Supper was administered, the table having been spread before the pulpit, the Elders, Deacons and heads of families first went up and partook of the symbolical bread and wine together, as handed them by the pastor; then the remainder of the congregation took their turn in sitting down at the Lord's table, till all had been served. After the ceremony, the bread and wine remaining was passed around among the poorer people who had come long distances, by way of refreshment, before they started for home. It was customary for many of the congregation to lunch out on the open green sward in front and on the south side of the church, after service.

XIII. THE SUCCESSORS OF DOM. MARINUS.

As already stated Dom. Marinus left this part of the country in 1773. But it seems that in 1762 the Conferentie party, anxious to get clear of Marinus, who was of the Cœtus party, called Dom. Cornelius Blauw to take charge of the churches at Totowa, Fairfield and Boonton (now Montville). He remained about five years, then removed to Hackensack, and died about 1770, after a three years' pastorate. He lived at Two Bridges, and having no carriage was taken to and from church by the more fortunate people. He is said to have been from Holland, a good preacher, but quarrelsome, "invading the congregations of others, accepting calls from the disaffected, and illegally administering the ordinances to them." He fell into irregular, dissipated habits at the last.

From 1767-'72 the Totowa pulpit appears to have been vacant, unless Dom. Marinus resumed his old pastoral relation, which is not improbable. However, in November, 1772, Pompton and Totowa called the Rev. Hermanus Meyer, D. D., and he was installed over those churches. Dr. Meyer was born in Bremen, Lower Saxony, July 27, 1733, of good parentage, and received an excellent education. In 1763 he was called to Kingston, N. Y., where he served with marked ability, but desiring to remain neutral between the Cœtus and the Conferentie he offended both, and a majority of the Consistory being of the latter party closed the church door against him, and repulsed him by an armed sentinel. He consequently had to minister for several years in private houses, until he was called to Totowa. In 1784 he was appointed Professor of Hebrew, and in 1786 Lector or Assistant to the Professor of Divinity; in 1789 Queen's (now Rutgers) College conferred on him the degree of D. D. He died at his residence at Pacquanac or at Two Bridges, after a brief illness, Oct. 27, 1791, widely lamented. He was a profound scholar and had begun a new translation of the Old Testament, but only completed the Psalms. He was buried under the pulpit of the Pompton church, and his remains have never been disturbed.*

"It is said that his last sermon was from the text, 'He that hath the Son hath life,' dwelling particularly on the last clause of the text, 'hath life.' He had contemplated administering the Lord's Supper two weeks from that day, but he was taken ill. During his sickness he sent for one of the Elders and gave him

---

*Sprague's Annals Reformed Dutch Church, pp. 31-6.

directions about his funeral. He only remarked, 'I meant to
have administered the Lord's Supper next Sabbath, but the
Lord has intended otherwise, and I shall not drink wine
again until I drink it in my Father's Kingdom.' As expressive
of his pious sentiments he remarked on taking a little refreshment, 'I have no more taste for what I once relished, but the
bread of heaven is provided for me.'" (*MS. of Rev. Dr.
John H. Duryea*, 1869.)

After the death of Dr. Meyer, the connection between Totowa and Pompton was dissolved, after thirty-five years dura-
tion, and the connection with Acquackanonk was renewed,
the two churches calling the Rev. Henricus Schoonmaker,
who was to preach one-third of the time in Totowa. Mr.
Schoonmaker was born in Rochester. Ulster County, N. Y.,
July 18, 1739, and was one of the first licensed by the Cœtus.
Hence his ordination was opposed by the Conferentie, who
managed to get possession of the church at Poughkeepsie,
where the ceremony was to take place, locked and barred it.
But his friends brought out a wagon under an apple-tree before
the church, and from that impromptu pulpit the Rev. John M.
Goetschius preached the sermon, and the candidate knelt there
and was ordained. He served very acceptably and with great
success, until his church required preaching in English, which
was beyond his power. Receiving a call in 1773 to Acquackanonk and Totowa he removed hither, and continued to preach
in Dutch till the last. In March, 1816, owing to the infirm-
ities of advancing age, he formally relinquished his charges
here, after forty-three years of successful labor. As a mark of
their appreciation the Acquackanonk Consistory voted him a
life annuity of $205. In the summer of 1816 he removed to
Jamaica, L. I., where he lived peacefully and happily with
his son, the Rev. Jacob Schoonmaker. "Here, in the blessed
hope of a glorious, immortal life, he terminated his earthly
career, in the eighty-first year of his age, on the 19th of January, 1820. His body was removed for burial among the people of his last charge, at Acquackanonk, and an impressive
funeral sermon was preached by the Rev. P. D. Freligh, then
the pastor of the church in that place, from Zachariah 1., 5."*

---

*Sprague's Annals of the Reformed Dutch Church, p. 39.

His son Daniel afterwards lived and died at what is now No. 172 Market street, Paterson. As remarked before, the good old man could not preach English. When John King's little daughter Grace (aged five years) died (Nov. 14, 1795), there being no other clergyman within several miles, Dom. Schoonmaker was invited to preach the funeral sermon. But what was the astonishment of the bereaved parents when the Dominie preached away in Dutch, of which they could understand very little! Small consolation could they get from his discourse, however comforting it might have been intended to be.

The Totowa church, which had hitherto had preaching only every third Sunday, now resolved (March 12, 1816) to have service every other Sabbath, if possible, and so notified the Acquackanonk Consistory, but that body seem to have taken time by the forelock, and March 20th notified the Totowa church that they had secured the services of the Rev. Peter Van Pelts, of Staten Island, and asked Totowa to take a third of his services. The Totowa church resolved that Acquackanonk had acted prematurely or *ex parte*, in not consulting Totowa, and repeated the demand for half the ministerial service; but on April 23, agreed to pay $300 a year for the pastor's salary, if he would preach one-third of the time at Totowa, and also give them services on the intervening Sunday afternoons, for eight months in the year, Totowa to be also exempt from the care or cost of the parsonage. But before this arrangement was consummated it was learned that the Rev. Wm. Eltinge, of Paramus, could be got for sixteen full Sundays in the year (Paramus agreeing), and that he likewise agreed to give his six free Sabbaths, making a total of twenty-two Sabbaths in the year, besides two holiday sermons, Totowa to pay $300 a year. A proposition was also received from the First Presbyterian church at Paterson to this effect: If Totowa would pay $250 ("less than one-third of the salary") toward the support of the Rev. Samuel Fisher, Mr. F. would act as their minister in visiting the sick, attending funerals, visiting the schools, and catechising the children, and would preach at Totowa every other Sunday, while the Totowa people would also have the privilege of attending the Presbyterian church. This

offer was declined, and after some further negotiation Mr. El-
tinge was secured, on the above terms.	He always preached
in English.

XIV. A Tragic Incident.

The proposal just mentioned, from the First Presbyterian
Church, recalls an earlier occasion when English was preached
in the old Totowa church, perhaps for the first time—an occasion connected with the most romantically tragic incident in the
history of the Passaic Falls.	The Presbyterians of the little
town had from time to time been favored with a service in English, and by the year 1812 had become so numerous that they
thought themselves entitled to regular preaching.	Application
was accordingly made to the Presbytery of Orange, and that
body recognized Paterson as a a mission station, and assigned
certain preachers to officiate there at regular intervals.	Among
those so assigned was the Rev. Hooper Cumming, pastor of the
Second Presbyterian Church of Newark.	Mr. Cumming was a
brilliant young man, the son of Gen. John N. Cumming, of
Newark, who had been an officer in the Revolution, afterwards
owner of an important line of mail coaches, and had built the
first raceway in Paterson.	Gen. Cumming was one of the lead-
ing citizens of Newark, his son was a graduate of Princeton, of
marked ability and engaging manners, a favorite in society,
and one of the most promising young clergymen in New Jersey.
About six weeks before coming to Paterson to fulfil the assign-
ment of Presbytery he had been united in marriage to Miss
Sarah Emmons, of Portland, Me., a young lady spoken of as
attractive in person and charming in manners, and but twenty-
two years of age.	It is not unlikely that Mr. Cumming thought
the trip to Paterson on ministerial duties might be utilized as a
continuation of his wedding journey, and doubtless his fond
young wife was glad enough to accompany her husband where
she was sure she would witness new triumphs of his eloquence,
and where she would, in his society, enjoy novel and beauti-
ful scenery.	We can see in fancy, their delightful drive one Sat-
urday afternoon, in June, along that charming road from Newark to Acquackanonk, by the riverside, and so on to Paterson,

where they were cordially welcomed by Mr. Samuel Colt, in his spacious mansion on Market street, near Main, where the Masonic Hall now stands. On Sunday morning, June 21st, 1812, the bell of the Totowa church clanged out notice that services were to be held that day. It was not the regular Sunday for Dominie Schoonmaker's ministrations, and the use of the church had been kindly given to the Presbyterians on this occasion, no doubt to the gratification of many of the congregation who longed for a sermon in English. Here is a description of the service, from the vivid and imaginative pen of Peter Archdeacon, as published in his "Sketch of the Passaic Falls," in 1845. Mr. Archdeacon did not come to Paterson until several years after 1812, so that his information was necessarily derived from others, but what he lacked in personal knowledge he made up in fertile fancy. Says this veracious chronicler:

"He was brilliant as an orator, and seemingly sincere as a Christian; the congregation was delighted with his discourse, his lady was beautiful and possessed virtues in an eminent degree that smooth the rugged path of life and soften the pillow to divine repose. The concluding words of his discourse were: 'Oh, ye people of Israel, why will ye not return?' The accent yet hung on his tongue when a blackbird was seen, and with trepidation flew all around and alighted on the pulpit, over the preacher's head. All eyes were turned to this ominous bird. The preacher in silence viewed the agitated throng, all inspired with divination, but none the point could fix. The next day alas! before the sun had veiled his head behind yon western hill, the flush was nipped, and the lovely seraph's spirit fled to the regions of the blessed! A melancholy gloom overspread the village; the silence of death seemed to pervade; few could give utterance to their thoughts; the mysterious appearance of the bird, thought some, was the harbinger of death; we turn, the angel to conduct her to the mansions of the blest."

It is scarcely necessary to say that the story of the blackbird was an invention of Mr. Archdeacon.

The tale is sad enough when simply told. On Monday morning, June 22d, the day after preaching in the Totowa church, Mr. Cumming and his young wife visited the Passaic

Falls, then in their pristine beauty. Tradition says that he was anxious to hasten back to Newark, and gave a reluctant assent to his wife's desire to visit the Falls. After viewing the scene from various points, together they crossed the narrow chasm to the precipice on the northwest side of the basin. Having looked he stepped back across the chasm, supposing she was close behind him. Looking around, she was gone! It is supposed that she had turned to take a second view, became dizzy and fell over the lofty precipice, here ninety feet in height. Her body was not recovered until the next morning, and was buried the day after, at Newark. Mr. Cumming's mind sustained a shock from which he never recovered, as his subsequent sad and varied career showed.

XV. Reconstruction of the Old Church.

When Dom. Schoonmaker left, a "party of progress" seems to have arisen in the church, and resolved that the old things should pass away. At the same meeting that his resignation was received (March 12, 1816), it was resolved to become incorporated under the act of 1799. Also, to repair the church. Also, "that the present pews be vacated and thrown into common, and that the present pews be equitably appraised by the Committee to be appointed to inspect and examine the church, and determine what alterations and repairs are necessary," the present value of the old pews to be credited on the purchase of the new ones. The following general committee was appointed: John Joseph Blauvelt, Abraham Godwin, Edo P. Merselis, John Doremus, John Van Blarcom, Cornelius Van Winkle, David Benson, Abraham Van Blarcom, John Berdan, Jacob Van Houten, Abraham V. Houten, Albert V. Saun, Edo Merselis, John G. Ryerson, Andrew Ackerman. Adrian Van Houten, Garabrant Van Houten, Esq., and Henry Godwin were "appointed Managers to carry into prompt and immediate effect the determination of a majority of the committee," and to superintend the work. After deliberating two or three times within the next few days, the alterations were agreed upon, a sketch being made by Abraham Godwin, Jr. The work was driven ahead with all dispatch and completed within

the next four months. The old floor was ripped up (by voluntary laborers in the congregation) and a new one thirteen inches higher put in ; more light was obtained by putting a fanlight
over the door (sidelights beside the door were also authorized,
but not put in) ; the old pews and side-benches were replaced
by two double rows of pews much shorter than the others, and
not so high by three inches, and a single row on each side under the galleries, in place of the side benches ; the galleries
were put in good repair, and instead of the open railing a panel
face was put in (the railing doing service for many years after
as a picket fence in John Joseph Blauvelt's garden, on Totowa) ; the interior was painted white. The colored people were
now assigned the forward part of the northerly gallery, and
there sat. It was proposed to fit up pews in the galleries, but
this was not done. The repairs and alterations having been
substantially completed, the church was opened on Sunday,
July 14, 1816, when the Rev. Wilhelmus Eltinge preached his
first sermon therein, it being "an excellent discourse from
Psalm xxvii, 4 ; 'One thing have I desired of the Lord, that
will I seek after ; that I may dwell in the house of the Lord all
the days of my life, to behold the beauty of the Lord, and to
inquire in his temple.'" (*Minutes.*) On Saturday, July 27th,
the pews were sold ; there were sixty-six pews, holding from
four to six persons, and they brought the very handsome total of
$2,056.

Thenceforward the church enjoyed a quiet and rather successful career for eleven years. True, there was something of a
"breeze" occasioned in 1825, by Mr. Brant Van Blarcom, of
Paterson, submitting to the Consistory and congregation a written document in which he strongly urged the need of having a
pastor settled regularly at Totowa or at Paterson. And he proposed that a new church be organized in Paterson, to be governed by the Totowa Consistory or by one of its own, and that
a pastor be secured to serve both congregations, preaching alter-
nately on either side of the river. To this end he offered to give
a seven years' lease of "the double-house in Parke street, next
north Robertson's watchmaker shop," (where A. & J. Spear's
shoeshop now is, No. 93 Main street), the yearly rental of which

was $260, and friends offered to furnish the house for a parsonage. His offer he considered equivalent to $350 a year. It is understood that Mr. Van Blarcom wanted to get the Rev. Benjamin C. Taylor, then at Acquackanonk, called to Paterson and Totowa. The Totowa congregation seem to have been very angry at Mr. Van Blarcom's offer, and declared that they were satisfied with Mr. Eltinge, and " resolved, that we are not yet ready to sell our minister and our souls for the sum of $350 per annum for seven years."

XVI. Pew Holders in 1816.

The following is a report of the sale of pews after the reconstruction of the interior of the church in 1816, showing the number of each pew, the number of sittings in each, the purchaser or purchasers, and the price paid:

Pew No. 1, 8 seats, two seats bought by John D. Ryerson, for $5. (Four seats were reserved to Henry Brockholst's heirs, in accordance with the deed of 1762.)

No. 2—4. Wm. Ferguson, $11.

No. 3—5. Daniel Benson, $22.

No. 4—4. Hartman Van Norder and Cornelius Westervelt, each two seats, $17.

No. 5—5. Jacob I. Van Houten, three seats, Francis Van Winkle, two seats. $29.

No. 6—4. Richard Van Gieson and Halmech R. Van Houten, each two seats, $17.

No. 7—6. David Bensen, $32.

No. 8—4. Albert Terhune, $17.

No. 9—5. Daniel Van Horn, $37.

No. 10—4. Edward Mitchell, $21.

No. 11—5. Edo P. Merselis, $41.

No. 12—4. Richard H. Van Houten, $21.

No. 13—5. Albert Van Saun. $39.

No. 14—4. Edo Merselis, $20.

No. 15—5. John Doremus and Abram Ryerson, each two and a half seats, $45.

No. 16—4. Cornelius C. Van Houten and Peter A. Van Houten, each two seats, $30.

No. 17—5. Henry G. Doremus, $46.

No. 18—6. Albert Van Houten, Adrian Van Houten and Rachel Van Houten, $21.

No. 19—6. Adrian and Halmech Van Gieson, each three seats, $25.

No. 20—6. Roelof I. Van Houten, $22.

No. 21—6. Robert Van Houten, five seats, Anna Van Houten, one, $33.

No. 22—6. Cornelius Van Houten, $34.

No. 23—6. Adrian R. Van Houten, $40.

No. 24—6. John Joseph Blauvelt and Isaac I. Stagg, each two, $40.

No. 25—6. Abraham R. Van Houten, $11.

No. 26—5. Cornelius Van Winkle, $45.

No. 27—5. Abraham Van Blarcom, $72.

No. 28—6. Abraham Godwin and Abraham Godwin Jr., each three seats, $32.

No. 29—6. Peter Van Allen and Peter Van Allen, Jr., each three seats, $42.

No. 30—6. Edo Merselis, $30.

No. 31—6. Albert Hopper and Cornelius P. Hopper, each three seats, $30.

No. 32—6. Hartman M. Vreeland, Adrian I. Post and Elizabeth Post, two each, $33.

No. 33—6. John Burhans and Hassel H. Doremus, each three seats, $19.

No. 34—6. John Seager and John Burhans, each three seats, $16.

No. 35— ——. John Marinus and David Marinus, $11.

No. 36—4. Thomas Wills, Jr., $32.

No. 37—5. Francis D. Ryerson and Richard Degray, each half, $40.

No. 38—4. Andrew Parsons, $21.

No. 40—4. Daniel Holsman, $40.

No. 41—5. Cornelius Vreeland, three seats, and Garabrant Van Rypen, two, $40.

No. 42—4. Charles Kinsey, $19.

No. 43—5. John S. Van Winkle and John I. Berdan, each half, $35.

No. 44—4. Martynus Hogencamp, $19.

No. 45—5. John C. Van Ryper and Halmech Van Houten, each half, $32.

No. 46—4. Jeremiah Tier, $19.

No. 47—5. Andrew Ackerman, $26.

No. 48—4. Aaron King, Robert King and John Flood, each a third, $19.

No. 49—5. John Goetschius, $25.

No. 50—4. John F. Post, two, John M. Crosson, one, and Ann Van Blarcom, one, $20.

No. 51—5. Cornelius Van Blarcom, ——.

No. 52—8. Jacob I. Van Houten, ——.

No. 53—5. Edo Van Winkle and John Parke, each half, $27.

No. 54—5. Jerry S. Van Rypen, $29.

No. 55—5. Geo. I. Ryerson, $35.

No. 56—5. John R. Van Houten and Richard Berdan, each half, $30.

No. 57—5. John Degray, $48.

No. 58—5. John Van Blarcom, $54.

No. 59—5. Simeon Van Winkle, $60.

No. 60—5. Peter Merselis, $59.

No. 61—5. Adrian Van Houten, $77.

No. 62—2½. Abraham C. Zabriskie, $40; 2½ seats reserved to the church.

No. 63—5. Garabrant Van Houten, $77.

No. 64—5. B. & J. Van Blarcom, each half, $71.

No. 65—5. John Joseph Blauvelt, $55.

No. 66—5. Abraham V. Houten, $60.

Total receipts from pews sold, $2,056.

Several of the foregoing pew-holders of course were of other denominations,—as William Ferguson, John Seager, Thomas Wills, Jr., Andrew Parsons, Daniel Holsman, Charles Kinsey, Aaron King, Robert King, John Flood, John Parke, and probably others—but bought pews in this church and perhaps attended its services regularly because there were only two other church organizations in the neighborhood, and they were very feeble—the First Presbyterian of Paterson, and an embryo M. E. church, meeting wherever it could find a room.

XVII. Statistics.

There are no statistics known to be extant relative to the Totowa church, prior to 1812. In that year it reports 111 families and 78 members. In 1817 there were 130 families and 67 members in communion; in 1821—175 families of 1105 persons, 105 members, 36 having joined during the year on profession of their faith; in 1823—179 families, 1125 persons, 110 members, 43 joining on profession; in 1824—180 families, 1130 persons, 125 members, 13 accessions; in 1825—180 families, 1140 persons, 117 members, no accessions; in 1826—180 families, 1150 persons, 129 members, 9 accessions; in 1827—170 families, 1100 persons, 134 members, 5 accessions; in 1828—125 families, 575 persons, 88 members, 4 accessions; in May, 1830—100 families, 600 persons, 95 members, 5 accessions.

XVIII. " God's Acre."

Such is the tender and poetic name by which the Germans designate the grounds set apart for the sepulture of their dead. Applied to the old Totowa plot it was mathematically correct, the grounds being exactly an acre in extent. As was customary, the first interments were made nearest the church, but in the course of forty years the whole lot east and south of the church was filled with graves. A great many were without any other headstone than a smooth fragment of a field-stone, a foot or two square, generally with no mark on, but sometimes with initials or a date rudely carved on the hard surface. Brownstone slabs were rare hereabout in those days. The graveyard, extending easterly almost to the brook, has been built over now for fifty years or more, not a few skeletons having been unearthed in the digging of cellars, while whatever headstones there were have mostly been worn away doing duty as walks, door-steps and the like. In 1795 this part of the church lot was quite filled with graves, and the lot southwest of the Totowa road (Ryle avenue) was brought into requisition for burial purposes, the first interment being that of Grace King, aged five years, daughter of John King, sister of the late Aaron King, and aunt of the late Griffith King. There was a stone over the grave of Jane Van Winkle, aged two months, died 1791, but the infant was doubtless removed thither when its mother was buried in 1807. The following are some of the inscriptions copied from headstones in this ground about 1873, by the writer :

Children of Eben'r & Eliza'th Blachly, Deceased are NANCY, born July 7th, 1783, died Octobr. 9th, 1783, Aged 3 Months & 2 days. Also, JULIANNA, born August 11th, 1791, died July 3d, 1798, Aged 6 years, 11 Months & 23 days.

In Memory of JAMES KEANE, who died November the 1st, 1805, A native of Galway in Ireland, Aged 45 Years.

In Memory of Abraham Van Houten, son of Adrian Van Houten and Mary his wife, who departed this life July 28th, 1804, aged 29 Years, 7 Months and 12 days.

In Memory of Richard, son of Adrian Van Houten, who departed this life the 25th February 1806, aged 18 Years, 9 Months and 25 days.

In Memory of Leah, daughter of Adrian Van Houten, who departed this life March the 10th, 1806, aged 33 Years, 6 Months and 11 days.

In Memory of Adrian, son of Adrian Van Houten, who departed this life March the 16th, 1806, aged 21 Years, 3 Months and 3 days.

In Memory of Jacob Ackerman, who departed this life January the 20th, 1812, aged 65 years, 9 Months and 29 days.

[S]ARAH [the] wife of [TIMOTHY] B. Crane, [and] daughter of Luke [Snedek]er and Sarah Snedek]er his wife, who departed this life 18th January, 1824, aged 42 years.

In Memory of Margaret Hunter, Sister of Isabella King, who died December 21st, 1824, Aged 86 Years.

In Memory of John Ryerson, who died January 25th, 1835, aged 43 years, 3 months and 29 days.

In Memory of Mary Marvin, consort of Doct. Jonathan D. Marven, died May 23, 1810, aged 19 years.

Lucreehe Stagg, daughter of Isaac Stagg, died Jan. 1st, 1829, aged 17 years.

Sarah, wife of John Mowerson, died April 11, 1803, aged 57 years. " Her death was suden and unexpected to her and to her friends."

Here lies all that is or was mortal of Susan Davis, second daughter of Abram and Mary Godwin, who departed this life Oct. 21, 1813.

In Memory of Genl. Abram Godwin, a soldier of the Revolution, died Oct. 5th, 1835, aged 72 years, 2 months and 19 days. Also Mary Munson Godwin, his wife, died Feb. 6th, 1826, aged 62 years, 7 months and 11 days.

In memory of Edo Merselis Godwin, son of Henry and Mary Godwin, died Oct. 8th, 1813, aged 3 months, 20 days.

In one corner was a large tomb, the stone lintel bearing this inscription :

"Owners of this vault—Cornelius Van Winkle, Richard Ward, Abram Van Houten, Albert Van Sann. October 9, 1813."

Gen. Godwin, who died in 1835, was one of the last interred in this now sadly-neglected spot. Many families long ago removed their dead from this cemetery, leaving the headstones still standing. In the spring of 1888, the First Reformed church had all the remains yet in the old burying-ground taken up and re-interred in the cemetery of the church on Willis street. Here is the only reference to the burying-ground that we find in the Church Records :

June the 21——18'3.

At a Meting of the Duch consistory of the totoway church have unanimous A greed that Every Person is to Pay for Laying and to Be Buyried in this Church yard, to Pay the Sum of for Twelve years and upwards is to Pay the Sum of one Dollar and under Twelve years the Sum of fifty Cents.

XIX. Burning of the Old Church.

On a dry and windy day, on March the 26th, 1827, the town of Paterson was startled by the cry of fire ! The two hand engines, primitive affairs, were quickly got out and hurried to the scene of destruction—the quaint old Totowa church. But there was no saving the old building, the cedar shingles of which were dry as tinder, and in the course of an hour nothing but bleak and blackened walls remained of the building so fraught with rich, varied and tender memories, and reminiscences of the wars in the church culminating in the independence of the Reformed Dutch Church of America, and of wars of the nations, many a stirring incident of which had occurred within sight of its belfry and which had resulted in a nation's freedom. As the crowd stood helplessly by, the old bell which had rung for nearly three-quarters of a century, now wept great tears of metal as the pitiless flames slowly and savagely crawled up and around it, wreathing it in their merciless embrace until at last it fairly wept itself away, and the whole roof fell in with a crash. An event of such interest happening to-day would furnish the reporters with material for a column or two of "fine writing," historical reminiscences and the like, but here is all that the Paterson *Intelligencer* thought it worth while to say about the fire on the Wednesday following:

Fire.—About eleven o'clock, A. M. on Monday last the roof of the Reformed Dutch Church in this town was discovered to be on fire. The wind at the time was pretty high, from the southwest, and before the fire engines could arrive the roof had become almost an entire sheet of flame; and so rapid was the progress of the destructive element, that in less than half an hour the whole wood work of the building became a heap of smoking ruins.

A burning flake carried by the wind from the church, lodged on the thatched roof of the barn belonging to Garabrant Van Houten, Esq., several hundred yards distant, which was also entirely consumed.

Much credit is due to our fire companies, and citizens generally for their prompt and successful exertions to save the adjacent buildings, which, from their combustible materials, and the direction of the wind, were in imminent danger, and seemed to threaten a most extensive conflagration.

The fire is supposed to have originated from the carelessness of some person shooting, the wadding having lodged on the roof and communicated to the shingles.

It is said that some person shot at a bird on the roof, and the wadding lodged between the shingles.

The desolate walls remained standing for nearly a year, and were then removed to enter into the construction of the new edifice, on Main street, near Ellison, which was contracted for March 8th, 1828.

The old lot was leased for a few years, but finally all that part of it northeast of the Totowa road, now Ryle avenue, was sold and is now built upon, over the graves of the dead now interred there for nearly a century and a quarter. And thus disappeared the last vestige of the OLD DUTCH CHURCH OF TOTOWA.

Of the events which succeeded the calamity above described we need not speak at length. Suffice it to say that while the congregation seemed to be quite unanimous as to the inexpediency of rebuilding on the old site, they were very much divided on the question of a new site, a large party preferring to remain north of the river, while another large party preferred building in the then growing town of Paterson. The pastor and all but one or two of the Consistory favored the latter

4

course, which was ultimately adopted by vote of the congregation. In consequence of this decision Messrs. Gerrebrandt Van Houten, Martinus I. Hogencamp, John Joseph Blauvelt, Adrian R. Van Houten, Cornelius S. Van Wagoner, David Bensen and Cornelius G. Hopper notified the Consistory (Aug. 23, 1827), with assurances of the kindliest feeling, that they would petition Classis in the following month to constitute them a new church, and hence the Second Reformed church, corner of Water and Temple streets, which edifice, by the way, was completed and opened for public worship on Sunday, June 8, 1828, while the Main street church was not dedicated until March 15, 1829.

Judge Gerrebrandt Van Houten gave the site for the Second church, contributed liberally of his means towards its erection, and had concluded to pay off a debt of about $2,000 remaining on it, but died suddenly of apoplexy the night after he had announced his benevolent intention.

The fire and the subsequent unhappy divisions had a depressing effect on the worthy and zealous Dominie Eltinge, the extent of whose depression may be inferred from the following note, appended to his statistical report to Classis in September, 1827. He says :   •

> The additions to our church during the year past have been small, only six have been added, these, however, gave very satisfactory evidence of a real change. As a congregation we are at present much afflicted, our house of worship has been consumed by fire, and we are divided as to the site for the new church. "By *the River Passaic* (!) we have reason to sit down, and weep when we remember Zion, and to hang our harps upon the willows in the midst thereof." By order of the Consistory of Totowa.

It may be remarked that the stone set in the wall over the door of the old church, and bearing the legend and date already given, was carefully preserved and placed in the belfry of the Main street church, where it was undoubtedly destroyed in the fire of December 14, 1871.

XX. Supplementary Notes.

The critical reader has doubtless noticed a conflict of dates relative to the settlement of Dom. Schoonmaker over Totowa, and the time of service of Dom. Meyer. It is probable that Dom. Schoonmaker's settlement at Acquackanonk and subsequent long service in both churches, 1791–1816, led his biographer quoted above (from *Sprague's Annals*), to suppose that his pastorate over each congregation was coequal throughout; but he is clearly in error, as the Classical records extant show that Dr. Meyer was pastor of Totowa, in connection with Pompton, 1773–'91.

A Sunday school was organized in connection with the church, as early as 1825. December 19, of that year, " Mr. Brant Van Blarcom, one of the Superintendents, laid before the Consistory his accompts for books bought for the Sunday school under the care of this church, amounting to $46.27½, less $11.14 advanced to him," and he was allowed the balance. It is probable that these were the first books bought for the school. The Sunday school was held in a low frame building, twenty or thirty feet in the rear of the church, erected about 1810 for a schoolhouse. It was not much injured by the fire of 1827.

With these fragmentary notes, gathered up at odd intervals during many years, amid other more engrossing occupations, ends the history of the OLD DUTCH CHURCH AT TOTOWA.

And yet, does it ? Who can tell what subtle influences that old church still exerts upon the population of Paterson and the surrounding country? While it stood it was a bulwark, a "strong fortress" of earnest piety and staunch orthodoxy. The leaven thus generated permeated the whole of society hereabouts, and it is not easy to believe that its power is even now exhausted. While it stood, and especially while the preaching was in Dutch, it was a visible sign of the ancient supremacy of that people, and gave them a moral prestige they could not otherwise have retained so long.

The quaint old stone building is indeed no more, but the Truth therein proclaimed for seventy-two years shall endure forever.

APPENDIX.

NOTE A.

The only baptismal register of the old church that is known to exist is an oblong volume, bound in parchment, sixteen inches long and six inches wide, containing eighty-two leaves or one hundred and sixty-four pages. The title is in the handwriting of Dominie Marinus, as is also the New Call made to him in 1752, written in a fine, round hand. The subsequent entries have been evidently written by various persons. The ink is faded; in a few cases the writing is undecipherable. In time the book will be destroyed, or the entries will be so faded that they cannot be read. To guard against such loss, and to make the information more available, it has been thought well to reproduce the contents of the volume herewith, verbatim et literatim, with an occasional note or translation by way of explanation.

Kerkelyk Protocol

der hervormde

Gemeynte Jesu Christi

tot Totua in de

County van Berge & Provintie

van Ooft Niew Jersey

in Noord America anno Domini

1756

David Marinus V: D: M:

Church Register of the reformed Church of Jesus Christ at Totua in the County
of Bergen Province of East New Jersey in North America A. D. 1756.

De Nieuwe Beroepsbrief van Do David Marinus tot Predikant op Achquechnonk Totua en Pomptan.*

In de name Gods !

Nadien dat de Nederduytsche Hervormde Gemeente in de tot nu toe vereenigde Plaadschen Achquechnonk en Pomptan in oost New Jersey in Noord America UErw Do David Marinus tot hunne Herder on Leeraer gehad hobben hebbende UErw: het Leeraers ampt seer eyverig en Godvruchtig reeds vier Jaaren onder ons waergenome met Loflyke Stigtinge so heeft het den Rykdom van Gods goedertierentheyd behaagt onse Gemeentens so danig door UErwaerdens dienst te doen groeje en Bloeje dat er Uyt de twee voormelde Gemeentens met algemeyne toestemminge van beyde een derde Gemeente ontstaen is tot Totua het welk ons genoodzaakt heeft onse voorgaende Beroepsbrief in Eenige van desselfs omstandig heeden te veranderen en tot dien Eynde zyn wy ouderlingen en Diaconen van de nu Drie gecombineerde Gemeentens van Achquechnonk Totua & Pomptan op vrydag den 23 April in het Jaar onses Heeren 1756 in de Kerk te Achquechnonk by een vergadert en hebben met zyn wel Eerw Do Reinhert Erickson alse onse Consulent Raadgepleegt en na aenroepinge van Gods Naem zyn wy Eyndelyk tot dit besluyt gekomen

1. Dat UErw de helft van de Predikdienst sult doen op Achquechnonk de vierde op Totua en de vierde op Pomptan

2. De H. Dagen in UErws eerst Beroepsbrief gemelt zullen gehouden-worden op die plaadschen daerse het naast by de zondag komen uytgenome Hemelvaardsdag die zalverstreckken tot een beurt in de Gemeonte in welke UErw die vieren zult

3. Het geheele Jaar door zult UErw op den dag des Heeren eens prediken Ses maenden op het Langst van de dagen zult UErw terstond na gedane Predikatie Catichiseeren in de Kerk hoedikwils UErw de aendere ses maenden des jaers Catichiseeren zult en waer zulks geschieden zal word gelate aen het goedvinden van UErw met UEkerkenraat gelyk het ook UErw met UEkerken-raad met de Catichisatien tot Slotterdam handelen zult

4. Tweemaal des Yaars zult UErw huysbesoekinge doen in de Gemeynte tot Achquechenonk Eens des jaars in de Gemeynte tot Totua en Eens in de Gemeynte tot Pomptan so lang UErws sichaems gesteltheyd zulks toelaaten viermaal des jaers zult UErw het H: Avondmael in jeder Gemeynte bedieno

---

*A translation of this document is given on pages 14–16. The spelling of Dutch words has been materially modified by modern lexicographers, and it does not seem that Dominie Marinus was strictly accurate in his orthography even according to the usage of his day.

5. Wanneer UE door siekte of aendersins eens van huys moeste weese so
sult UE de beurt moete waerneeme daese Soudags van te voren moest
waergenome worde en dit doende so belovenwy UErw op UE dienst onder ons
als bovegemelt

1. Een sjaerlyks Tractament van Hondert en Sestien Pouden New Jersey
Gelt tegen half Proclamatie gerekent of aanders Niewyorks gangbaer gelt
waervan UErw door de ouderlingen en Diacouen die nu zyn en van tyd tot
tyd na ons zullen in den dienst zyn alle half yaar de gerechte helft zal
betaalt worden dat is de E Kerkenraat van Achquechnonk zal u sjaerlyks agt
en vyftig Pouden de E Kerkenraad van Totua negen en Twintig pouden en de
E Kerkenraad van Pomptau negen en Twintig Pouden.

2 hier nevens een bequame woninge die ten tyden van Do Henricus Koens
op Achquechnonk niews getimmert is en Staat digt by de Kerk een Schuer voor
Paarden en Beesten, een put een thuynen Ses ackkers Land dit alles zullen we
Repareeren en in Reparatie houden dewelke met alles desselfs Beneficien en
Profyten de uwe zullen zyn so lange UE onse Leeraar syd   •

3. maer zo het mochte gebeure dat een of aender van de voormelde
gecombineerde Gemeyntens zoude wygeren ofte nalatig zyn haer Egale Part
na proportie van hun dienst diese genieten het zy in opsicht van voormelde
Tractament of in opsicht van voormelde Reparatie na te kome, so zullen
de aendere Gemeente of Gemeentens het volkome recht hebben de Dienst
van hunne Plicht niet nakomende Gemeynte over te neeme mits zydan ver-
plicht zulle zyn de bovengemelde Conditiente vervullen
En tot het nakomen van dit alles zo verplichten wy ons als teegenwoordige
ouderlingen en Diacone gelyk dat ook doen zullen allen en een jegelyk die
na ons van tyd tot tyd in den dienst tot ouderlingen en Diaconen onser
Gemeentens zullen beroepen worden en dat voor en aleer dat zy in hunne
bedieningen zullen bevestigt zyn te weete deese Beroepinge meede te
ondertykenen Jehovah God dan bidden wy laate deese onse beroepinge wel
gelukken en doese uytvalle tot eere en heerlykheyd van Gods Naem tot
uytbreydinge van zyn Koningryk en inwinninge en zaligheyd van veele
zielen amen!
aldus gedaen te Achquechnonk
den 23 april 1756
Ju tegenwoordigheyd van
Reynhert Erickson als consulent
Sie het origineele met de handtyconinge en het
Kerkelyk Protocol tot Achquechnonk.

Register der gedoopte Kinderen.*

Ouders | Hendrick Francisco | getuygen | Jacob Francisco
Marytje Snyer | | Antje Snyer
Naem Elizabeth gebore den 9 July gedoopt den 8 aug: 1756

Ouders | Helmich D: Van Houte | getuygen | Cornelus van Houte
Antje Post | | Fytje van Houte
Naem Elizabeth geboren den 23 Octob gedoopt den 27 octobris 1756

Ouders | Johannis Ryke | getuygen | Johannis Spier
Eva Sherman | | Lea Post
Naem Abraham gebore den gedoopt den 19 maert 1758

Ouders | Petrus vaness | getuygen | Johannis Pier
Hendrica Pier | | Hester vaness
Naem Marytje den 21 maert geboren en den 16 april gedoopt 1758

Ouders | Thomas mills | getuygen | Cornelus Westerveld jun
Majeke Post | | Jannitje vanHoorn
Naem Martha gebore den 8 Aug: ged. d 8 Sept 1758

Ouders | Hendrick Jacobusse | getuygen | Cornelus Spier
Sara Stynmetz | | Sophia Jacobusse
Naem Conelus gebore den 13 aug: gedoopt: den 3 Sept 1758.

Ouders | Niclaes Low | getuygen | Cornelus Low | naem
Sarah Low | | Arrijaentje Low |
Johannis gebor: den 7 Sept ged den 1 octob 1758

Ouders | Pieter Berry | getuygen | Jacobus Barjo | Naem
Susanna Jones | | Hester Berry |
Picter gebore den 1 Decem: gedoopt den 25 Dec: 1758

Corneliaus Low   Geboren de 21 September 1745

Ouders | yurye westervelt | getuygen | Pieter Post
Marritye gerritse | | Marregriet zyn vrou
Naem Cornelus geboren de 2 Mey gedoopt de 17 Mey 1760

Ouders | Cornelus van houten | getuygen | Johannes v. giese
Marretye v: giese | | Aeltye v. giese
Naem Lena geboren de 24 Novemb. gedoopt 25 Decmr. 1761

Ouders | hendrick Bruyn | getuygen | abraham Beem
Catriena Beem | | zyn huysvrou
Naem Sara gebooren de 17 June gedoopt 26 July 1761

Ouders | Samuel Rome | getuygen | Barent Kool
grietye Kool | | Sara Kool
Naem hendrick geboren 16 febr: gedoopt 12 April 1762

---

*"Register of baptized Children." *Ouders*, parents; *getuygen*, witnesses; *naem*, name of child; *gebore* or *geboren*, born; *gedoopt*, baptized; *Maart*, *Mert* or *Maert*, March; *Mey*, May. The first eight entries are in the handwriting of Dominie Marinus. The ninth is in the hand of one unaccustomed to writing. The subsequent entries are in a different chirography still. The pages of the original volume are not numbered, but a slight space is left in this printed book between the entries as written on each page of the record.

ouders | Johannis Cadmes | getuygen | hellimich v: houten
feytye v: houten | | Jannetye zyn vrou
Naem Cornelia   geboren 6 Mert   gedoopt   1762

onders | Pieter maudeviel | getuygen | hendrick Mandeveal
Maria Bertolf | | Marregrietye zy vrou
Naem Jan   geboren 19 Sept   gedoopt op Totowa 1762

Ouders | Johannis v: giesen | getuygen | Cornelis v: houten
Metye v: houten | | marytje zyn vrou
Naem Dirk   geboren 14 January   gedoopt 23 January 1763

Ouders | Dirck v: Rijpen | getuygen | gerrit v: Rijpen
Elisabeth meet | | Lena zyn vron
Naem Yurrie   geboren 26 Mert   gedoopt op totowa 1763

Ouders | Poules Rattan | getuygen | helmich v: houten
Jannetye Bord | | Eva zyn vrou
Naem Poulis   geboren 30 Maart   gedoopt op totowa 1763

Ouders | Dirck Ryerson | getuygen | Joris Ryerson
Lena Ryerson | | Antye hennion
Naem geertye   geboren 16 April   gedoopt op totowa 1763

Ouders | Jacobus Post | getuygen | Johannes Post
Metye gerritse | | Caterina v: houten
Naem Johannis   geboren 14 Mey   gedoopt op totowa 1763

Ouders | Johannis v: houten | getuygen | frans Post
Leybetye v: Reypen | | Catelyntye van houten
Naem yannetye   geboren 31 Octo.   gedoopt de 4 Decer. 1763.

Ouders | Teunes Dey | getuygen | De vader
Hester Schuylder | | & Moeder
Naem David   gebooren 30 November   gedoopt De 25 December 1763.

Ouders | Cornelus neefyes | getuygen | Johannes Neefyes
aeltye v: giesen | | Lena Dy
Naem Catelyntye   gebooren 10 December   gedoopt 25 Decem. 1763

Ouders | Barent Cool | getuygen | Mechiel koock
Cateryna Post | | en Selle Cool
Naem femmetye   geboren 28 January   gedoopt 26 febr. 1764

Ouders | Robbert Clark | getuygen | Jan lyn
grietye lyn | | Catrina lyn
Naem Marcytye   geboren 18 february   gedoopt De 18 van Mert 1764

Ouders | Cornelus van houten | | Robbert van houten
Marretye van giesen | | Elisabeth Post
| getuygen | Johannes van houten
Twelingen* | | Leybetye van Rypen
Naemen Der kinderen zyn De Een is genaemt Elisabeth en De andere
feytye   Gebooren Den 14 Mart   gedoopt De 8 van April 1764.

Ouders | Nicease Kip | getuygen | Hendrick Sisoo
Leya Mandeviel | | en zyn vrou
Naem Antye   gebooren De 25 May   gedoopt De 10 June 1764.

Ouders | gerrit gerritse . | getuygen | Hendrick gerritse
Ragel westervelt | | Zyn Moeder Marritye
Naem Marritye   gebooren De 1 Juni & gedoopt De 8 July 1764.

*"Twius. The names of the children are the one is named Elisabeth and the other Feytje."

Ouders | Poules Rutan | getuygen | Joris Bord
        | Iannetye bord | | Zyn Doghter Lena
Naem Antye gebooren De 14 July   gedoopt De 30 July 1764

Ouders | Johannes Neefyes | getuygen | Cornelus Neefyes
        | Leña Dy | | Aeltye van giesen
Naem gerrit gebooren De 25 September gedoopt De 14 October 1764

Ouders | Joris Ryerson | getuygen | Dirck Ryerson
        | Zyn vrou | | Lana Zyn vrou
Naem Antye gebooren De   gedoopt De 14 october 1764

Ouders | Direck Van Ripen | getuygen | Jacob Berry
        | Elizabeth meet | | Gretey meet
Naem Jacob gebooren De 2 January   gedoopt 27 January 1765

Ouders | France Post   · | getuygen | garret v Ripen
        | Catelyntye van houten | | Lena Syn vrow
Naem Mareytye gebooren 14 January   gedoopt 17 February 1765*

Ouders | Roelif v: houten | getuygen | Hessel Peterse
        | Antye hennion | | feytye v: houten
Naem Robbert geboren De 28 Mert   gedoopt De 1 Mey 1774

Ouders | Jan hopper | getuygen | Audries hopper
        | feytye Doorremus | | Catrina hopper
Naem Catrina gebooren De 7 april   gedoopt De 1 Mey 1774

Ouders | Jurre westervelt | getuygen | Steven bogert
        | Marretye gerretse | | geesye westervelt
Naem Steven geboren De 16 April   gedoopt De 22 Mey

Ouders | Hendrick v: Blercom | getuygen | Antoni v: Blercom
        | Annaetye v: wenkel | | Annaetye Koock
Naem vrouwetye geboren De 20 May   gedoopt De 29 May 1774

Ouders | Petrus v: houten | getuygen | Johannes v giesen
        | Leya v: Rypen | | Metye v: houten
Naem Elisabeth geboren De 13 May   gedoopt De 29 May 1774

Ouders | frans v: blercom | getuygen | De vader
        | Jackomyn v: horn | | En De Moeder
Naem Antoni geboren 8 July   gedoopt De 24 July

Ouders | Hessel Ryerson | getuygen | John gerritse
        | Doorte Earl | | geertye Ryerson
Naem geertye geboren 5 July   gedoopt De 24 July

Ouders | Johannis westervelt | getuygen | †
1774 | Elizabeth bogert | |
Naem grietye geboren 14 July   gedoopt De   Augustus

Ouders | Roelif v. houten | getuygen | Johannes v houten
1774 | Annaetye kip | | en zyn vrouw
Naem Johannes geboren De 29 July   gedoopt De 21 August

Ouders | Gerrit gerritse | getuygen | yurre westervelt
        | Marregrietye gerritse | | Marritye gerritse
Naem Johannes gebooren 18 September   Gedoopt 2 October 1774

*The nine pages following in the Register are blank, covering a period of as many years—1765 to 1774—when the record is resumed in the same handwriting as before, from which it may be inferred that part of the record was made up some years after the baptisms occurred.

†This entry and the one following are almost illegible, the ink having faded.

1774 | Nicknse v: blercom | getuygen | John v: blercom
Ouders | Catrienna Post | | Catrienna v: Rypen
Naem John   gebooren De 25 Septemb.   gedoopt 16 Octob.

1774 | henderick Merccker | getuygen | Johannes Cirris
Ouders | Maria Kranck | | Maria Jacobosse   •
Naem Johannis   geboren De 4 oc'ber   gedoopt De 30 oct'er

Ouders | Harmanes Meyer | getuygen | Johannis Hardenbergh
| Ragel Hardenbergh | | Maria du Bois
Kint Johannes Herdenbergh   gedoopt De 13 November   geboren De 19 October 1774

Ouders | hendrick Jacobusse | getuygen | Lyes Smit
| Lena v. blercom | | Maria Jacobosse
Naem Johannes gebooren De 15 october gedoopt De 13 November 1774

ouders | Jacob vreland | getuygen | Roelif v: houten
| geertye v:winkel | | antye hennion
Naem Hartman   gebooren 2 November   gedoopt De 13 November 1774

ouders | adman kingland | getuygen | Ester Dey
| polle | |
Naem Johannis geboren De   gedoopt De 13 November 1774.

Ouders | John Drummund | getuygen | Hendrick Spier
| Elisabeth Bruyn | | Polliy Drummond
Naem Nence   gebooren De 16 July   gedoopt De 21 Augustus 1774

Ouders | Jacob Doorremus | getuygen | Cornelus Doorremus
| Nieltye Pier | | Sara Ryerson
Naem Sara   geboren De 25 october   gedoopt De 4 December 1774

Ouders | Peter Post | getuygen | Adreyaen Jacobosse   •
| Geertye Jacobosse | | Polle van Rypen
Naem Marcke Gebooren De 28 November gedoopt De 18 December 1774

Ouders | Cornelus van winkel | getuygen | Waeling v: winkel
| Annaetye van Rypen | | Maria v: winkel
Naem Waeling gebooren De 2 December gedoopt De 18 December 1774

Ouders | Adreyaen van houten | getuygen | Dirk van houten
| Marretye Cadmus | | Ragel Newkerk
Naem Abraham   gebooren De 16 December   gedoopt De 26 December 1774

Ouders | Johannes Meedt | getuygen | Hendrick Demodt
| Marregrietye Demodt | | Cattalyntye Demodt
Naem Hendrick   gebooren De 13 December 1774   gedoopt De 15 January 1775

Ouders | Salomon van Debeek | getuygen | Albert terhuen
| geesye terhuen | | Sus van Derhoef
Naem Albert   gebooren de 27 Januari   gedoopt de 26 februari 1775

Ouder | Pryntye* van winkil | getuygen | Johannis v: winkel
| | | Jaunetye Ryerson
Naem Arreyaentye Post   gebooren De 6 January   gedoopt Den 27 february 1775

Ouders | David griffins | getuygen | Hendick kool
| Selle Cool | | Marregrietye godwin
Naem hendrick   gebooren De 14 februari   gedoopt De 12 van Mart 1775

*A curious resemblance here between the name and the sin of her of the "Scarlet Letter."

Ouders | Cornelus van houten | getuygen | Adreyaen v: houten
| Metye van houten | | Elisabeth v: houten
Naem gerrebrant gebooren De 24 februari gedoopt Do 12 Mert 1775

Ouders | Henri godwin | getuygen | helena bandt
| kete Bandt | |
Naem helena geboren De 20 Mart gedoopt De 9 April 1775

Ouders | Dirk van houten | getuygen | De vader
| Maria van Rypen | | en Moeder
Naem Jannetye gebooren De 31 Mert gedoopt De 17 April 1775

Ouders | Johannes Lambart* | getuygen | Nickase Kep
| arreyaentye Mandeviel | | Laya Mandeviel
Naem Laya gebooren De 4 April gedoopt De 30 April 1775

Ouders | Hendrick van nes | getuygen | Jilles Meedt
| Zyn vrou Rachal | | Zyn vrou
Naem Robbert gebooren De 15 April gedoopt De 30 April 1775

Ouders | william Drummond | getuygen | De vader en
| Annaetye Spier | | Moeder van het kint†
Naem Sara geboren De 18 van April gedoopt De 21 May 1775

Ouders | Adreyaen v: houten | getuygen | Cornelius v: houten 1775
| Elisabeth v: houten | | Metye v: houten
Naem yannetye gebooren De 7 May gedoopt De 28

Ouders | Jan van blercom | getuygen | Hendrick van blercom
| Catrienna van Rypen | | annaetye van winkel
Naem Johannes geboren De 17 May gedoopt De 28 1775

Ouders | Hendrick Dooremus | getuygen | Jacobus ackerman
| Egge van houten | | Elisabeth ackerman
Naem David gebooren De 25 July gedoopt De 27 1775 Augustus

Ouders | Samuel van Saen | getuygen | De vader &
| Leya Zobrisko | | Moeder
Naem Annaetye gebooren De 15 Agustus gedoopt De Eeyste 1 october
1775

Ouders | Hendrick Doorremus | getuygen | Cornelus Jacobusse
| Marregrietye van winkel | | Catrina gerritse
Naem geertye geboren De 22 agustus gedoopt De 15 october 1775

Ouders | Hendrick Spier | geteygen | Hendrick Spier
| Pol Drummond | | Debra Roome
Naem Hendrick gebooren De 22 September gedoopt De 15 october 1775

Ouders | Jores Doorremus | getuygen | De vader en
| Marregrietye westervelt | | Moeder
Naem Cornelus gebooren De 13 September gedoopt de 15 october 1775

Ouders | Tuenis Ryerson | getuygen | De Vader
| Marritye Ryerson | | en Moeder
Naem Marritye geboren De 3 October gedoopt Dè 29 october 1775

Ouders | Jan Ines | getuygen | Die vader
| Catryn Ryker | | en Moeder
Naem Hester gebooren De 4 September gedoopt de 12 November 1775

*The name may be Rambart, but the R seems to have an L written over it.
†The father and mother of the child,

5

Ouders | Jannetye van blercom | getuygen | Hendrick Jacobosse / Lena van blercom
Naem David geboeren De 2 october gedoopt De 26 September 1775 by adreyan van houten huys by De bruge*

Ouders | David hennion / Jackomynye kep | getuygen | Jacobos Jacobosse / Marritye kip
Naem Jacobos geboeren De 15 November gedoopt De 10 December 1775

Ouders | Hendrick gerritse / Elisabeth gerritse | getuygen | Johannes gerritse / Claesye gerritse
Naem Elisabeth geboeren De 27 Decemr 1775 gedoopt De 28 Jannary 1776

Ouders | Hendrick Meed / Maria kline | getuygen | Dirck van Rypen / Elisabeth Meed
Naem Elisabeth geboeren De 25 Decr: 1775 gedoopt De 28 January 1776

Ouders | Dirck van houten / Ragel Newkerck | getuygen | Helmigh van houten / Catrienna van houten
Naem Antye geboren De 10 february gedoopt De 25 February 1776

Ouders | Johannes Meed / Marregrietye Demodt | getuygen | Dirk v: Rypen / Elisabeth Meed
Naem Johannes geboeren De 5 Mert gedoopt de 7 April 1776

Ouders | Barnt Cool / Catriena van Dewaters | getuygen | Hendrick Cool / Sara van de water
Naem Sara geboeren de 3 May gedoopt De 12 May 1776

Ouders | Adreyaen van houten / yannetye Merselis | getuygen | Hessel Pieterse / feythe v: houten
Naem adreyaen geboeren De 4 May gedoopt De 26 May 1776

Ouders | Jacob Spier / Marregrietye vrederixse† | getuygen | hendrick Spier / Debra Roome
Naem herdrick‡ geboren De 3 June gedoopt De 16 June 1776

Ouders | Dirck van houten / Maria van Rypen | getuygen | Cornelis van houten / Metye van houten
Naem Antye geboeren De 11 September gedoopt De 22 September 1776

Ouders | Samuel van Saen / Leya Zabrisco | getuygen | Jan Zabrisco / kestijnye Zabrisco
Naem Jan geboeren De 19 September gedoopt De 6 october 1776

Ouders | Johannes van giesen / Metye van houten | getuygen | De vader en / Moeder
Naem Johannes geboren De 8 Siptember gedoopt De 6 October 1776

Ouders | Hendrick Merceker / Maria kraukheyd | getuygen | abraham krankheyd / Eva kirris
Naem Lena geboeren De 5 Agustus gedoopt De 20 october 1776

Ouders | Jan Merceker | getuygen | hendrick Merceker
Naem Jurre geboeren De 11 June gedoopt De 3 November 1776

---

* The child was baptized at Adrian Van Houten's house at the bridge.
†Fredericks.
‡Manifestly a *lapsus pennæ* for *Hendrik*, Henry.

Ouders | Nickasi v: blercom | getuygen | Hendrick hennion
katrienna past | | | Maria Romyn
 Naem franscoos gebooren De 25 october gedoopt De 17 November 1776

Ouders | Bensmen Quereau | getuygen | De vader
annaetye Bruyn | | | en Moeder
 Naem Elias gebooren De 14 July gedoopt De 17 November 1776

Ouders | Hendrick Jacobosse | getuygen | De vader
Lena van blercom | | | en Moeder
 Naem Marretye gebooren De october gedoopt De 1 Decembe 1776

Ouders | Cornelis van Derhoof | getuygen | Hendrick v: blercom
Mareet Cryser | | | Annaetye v: winkel
 Naem John gebooren De 28 Novemb 1776 gedoopt

Ouders | Jacobos Jacobosse | getuygen | Ari Sisko
Maria Sisko | | | Ragel Jacobosse
 Naem gerrit gebooren De 9 November gedoopt De 15 December 1776

Ouders | Hendrick van blercom | getuygen | De
Annaetye van winkel | | | Vader & Moeder
 Naem Maria gebooren De 5 December gedoopt De 25 December 1776

Ouders | Jacob van winkel | getnygen | Roelif van houten
Elsye keep | | | Antye hennion
 Naem Jannetye gebooren De 9 Decm. gedoopt De 25 Decm. 1776

Ouders | Simion van winkel | getuygen | Jacob van winkel
Antye Merselus | | | Vrouwetye gerritse
 Naem Jacob gebooren De 6 Decem. 1776 gedoopt De 5 Janr. 1777

Ouders | Isack van houten | getuygen | De Vader
Maria Post | | | en Moeder
 Naem Isack gebooren De 11 Decm. 1776 gedoopt De 5 Janr. 1777

Ouders | Cornelis v: winkel | getnygen | Johannes v: winkel
Annaetye v: Rypen | | | gerritye Sip
 Naem Stynye gebooren De gedoopt De 16 february 1777

Ouders | Hendrick Ackerman | getuygen | Peter post
Marregriet post | | | geerttruy Jacobosse
 Naem peter gebooren De 31 January gedoopt de 16 february 1777

Ouders | gerrit h gerritse | getuygen | Jacobus post
Marregriet gerritse | | | Antye gerritse
 Naem hendrick gebooren De 6 february gedoopt De 2 Maert 1777

Ouders | Jan Wyt | getuygen | hans keesstede
Elsye Vreland | | | en Zyn Vrou
 Naem gerrit gebooren De 16 December 1776 gedoopt De 2 Mert 1777

Ouders | Jacob vreland | getuygen | Jacob van winkel
geertye van winkel | | | vrouwetye gerritse
 Naem hartman gebooren De 15 Maert gedoopt De 6 April 1777

*Ouders | Mouris Mourisse | getnigen | Hendrik Jacobusse
Treintje Jacobusse | | | Hester van Nes.
 Naam Jan, geboren d. 17 Nov: 1776.

Ouders | Nicoklas Piter Bogert | getuygen | Adolph Walderom
Catrienna walderom | | | Catarina Bogert
 1777 Naem Anna

---

*This entry is in the handwriting of Dominic Schoonmaker.

Ouders | frans v: blercom | Andries v: horn
Jackomyn v: horn | Ragel v: horn
Naem Andris   geboren de 25 July   gedoopt De 10 Augustus 1777

ouders | Jan J Ryerson | getuygen | De vader
Elsye lesier | | en Moeder
Naem antye   geboren De 13 June   gedoopt De 10 Agustus 1777

Ouders | Peter D Bou | getuygen | hans h pier
Zosanna pier | | en Neeltye v: Nes
Naem Maria   geboren De 26 July   gedoopt De 24 Augustus 1777

Ouders | Jacob Dooremus | getuygen | hans pier
Neeltye pier | | Hester van Nes
Naem Hester   gebooren De 31 July   gedoopt De 24 Augestus 1777

Ouders | Hessel Ryerson | getuygen | Hessel piterse
Doose Erl | | feytye v: houten
Naem Hessel   gebooren De 22 September   gedoopt De 19 october 1777

Ouders | EDo Merselis | getuygen | De Vader
Arreyaenthe Sip | | en Moeder van het kint
Naem gerrit   gebooren De 1 Dagh van october   gedoopt De 19 octor 1777

Ouders | Peter hopper | getuygen | De vader en
Annetye Doorremis | | Moeder
Naem andries   gebooren De 4 october   gedoopt De 2 November 1777

Ouders | Johannes van winkel | getuygen | Johonnis Ryerson
Cattelyntye Ryerson | | Catelyntye Berre
Naem Cattelyntye   gebooren De 5 November   gedoopt De 16 November 1777

Ouders | Johannis Byvanck | getuygen | De vader en
Jannetye Hogelant | | Moeder
Naem Jannetye   gebooren De 14 November   gedoopt De 14 December 1777

Ouders | Roelif van houten | getuygen | hendrick Doorremus
Antye hennion | | Marregriet hennion
Naem Johannes   gebooren De 2 Decm.   gedoopt De 25 Decm. 1777

Ouders | John Luewes | getuygen | De vader
Catryn Ryker | | en Moeder
De Namen De Enen Elisabeth De anderen feytye   gebooren De 13 November   gedoopt De 25 December 1777

Ouders | Ducelis Cernes | getuygen | De Vader en
geesye boskerk | | Moeder
Naem William   gebooren De 24 November 1777   gedoopt de 11 January 1778

Ouders | Johannes :v: winkel | getuygen | Waleng :van winkel
gerritye Sip | | Maria van winkel
Naem Helmigh gebooren De 14 December   gedoopt De 25 January 1778

Ouders | Hendrick :v: giesen | getuygen | Peter Wilson
Hendricke banta | |
Naem Zara   gebooren De 4 December   gedoopt De 25 January 1778

Ouders | Jacob van houten | getuygen | Isack van houten
Ragel Ackerman | | Maria post
Naem Jannetye   gebooren De 27 December   geDoopt De 25 January 1778

Ouders | Cornelus :v: houten | getuygen | Adreyaen :v: houten
Metye :v: houten | | Elisabeth :v: houten
Naem gerrebrant geboren De 18 January gedoopt De 8 february 1778

Ouders | thomas Parsells | getuygen | Joseph Morgan
Elenor Parsells | | Ragel van Iderstin
Naem Johannes Morgen geboren De gedoopt De 8 february 1778

Ouders | Salomon van Debeek | getuygen | Isack van Debeek
geesye terhune | | Ragel Ryerson
Naem Jannetye geboren De 8 January gedoopt De 1 Mart 1778

Ouders | Roelif van houten | getuygen | Cornelis van houten
Marregriet Shearer | | Sara Demarest
Naem Cornelis geboren De 15 September 1776 gedoopt de 1 Mart 1778

Ouders | Johannes Ryker | getuygen | Niccolas Ryker
Martynye Doorremus | | Marritye Bruyn
Naem Niccoles geboren De 30 January gedoopt De 1 Mart 1778

Ouders | Adreyeen van houten | getuygen | Helmigh H van houten
Marretye Cadmus | | Catrienna van houten
Naem Antye geboren de 21 Mert gedoopt De 12 April 1778

Ouders | Dirk van houten | getuygen | Johannes van giesen
Ragel Neukerk | | Metye van houten
Naem Helmigh geboren De 19 Mert gedoopt De 12 April 1778

Ouders | Dirk g van houten | getuygen | De Vader en Moeder
Maria van Rypen |
Naem Abraham geboren De 23 Mert gedoopt De 12 April 1778

Ouders | Theophilus Browr | getuygen | Henderick Spier
Maria Bogert | | Debora Roome
Naem Maria geboren De 18 April gedoopt De 17 Dagh May 1778

Ouders | Jacobos post | getuygen | frans post
Selle Dy | | Cattelyntye v: houten
Naem frans geboren De 22 May gedoopt De 21 June 1778

Ouders | Jan Dobs | getuygen | Abraham v: houten
Annaetye Ryerson | | Annaetye Wesselse
Naem Annaetye geboren De 7 June gedoopt De 5 July 1778

Ouders | Charls Sldde foolwood | getuygen | Jacob Bardan
feytye Boskerk | | Rebecke Ryerson
Naem Rebecke geboren De 29 June gedoopt De 19 July 1778

Ouders | Johannes Post | getuygen | Roelif v: houten
Catrienna van houten | | antye hennion
Naem Robbert geboren De 3 Augustus gedoopt De 30 Augustus 1778

Ouders | Bornt kool | getuygen | David Griffins
katrienna van De water | | Sara van De water
Naem Catrina geboren De 3 october gedoopt 25 october 1778

ouders | Johannes h gerritse | getuygen | Cornelis Jacobosse
Maria Zobrisko | | Catrina gerritse
Naem Catrina geboren De 20 September gedoopt De 25 october 1778

Ouders | Johannes D hennion | getuygen | Cornelis hennion
Catlynye Demod | | Eva hennion
Naem David geboren De 21 october gedoopt De 8 November 1778

Ouders | Cornelis haring | getuygen | De
Annetye ariyanse | | vader en Moeder
Naem ari geboren De october gedoopt De 22 November 1778

Ouders | Marten Myer | getuygen | De vader
Bregge ackerman | | en Moeder
Naem Leya gebooren De 26 November 1778 gedoopt De 1 January 1779

onders | Johannes Romyn | getuygen | Henderick Bertolf
Sara van winkel | | Neuse van winkel
Naem Benyamen gebooren De 17 November 1778 gedoopt De 10 January 1779

Ouders | Antoni van blarcom | getuygen | Johannes Post
Annaetye koock | | Catrina van houten
Naem Catrina gebooren De 17 December 1778 gedoopt De 24 January 1779

Ouders | Welliem Coerte | getuygen | De
Catrina Winter | | Vader en Moeder.
Naem Williem gebooren De 19 Decm 1778 gedoopt De 24 January 1779

) Ouders | Jacobus Couwenover | getuygen | Cristeyaen Demere*
en Zyn wyf | | Annaetye van hooren
Naem Cristeyaen gebooren De 7 January gedoopt De 24 January 1779

Ouders | Metys ackerman | getuygen | Cornellis v: houten
Maritye van houten | | Metye v: houten
Naem Polle gebooren De   gedoopt De 24 January 1779

Ouders | Adreyaen Post | getuygen | leyes Speer
Sara spier | | lena Jacobosse
Naem leya gebooren De 31 December 1778 gedoopt De 7 februari 1779

Ouders | Nickase van blercom | getuygen | Jan van blercom
katrienna post | | katrienna van Rypen
Naem Jan gebooren De 17 January gedoopt De 7 february 1779

Ouders | Mattheus van Derhoef | getuygen | De
Elisabeth beunet | | vader en Moeder
Naem Matthens gebooren De 21 November 1776 gedoopt De 5 July 1778

Ouders | Mattheus van Derhoef | getuygen | De
Elisabeth bennet | | vader en Elisabeth van houten
Naem Elisabeth gebooren De 20 January gedoopt De 21 february 1779

Ouders | george Ryerson | getuygen | De
polle Ryerson | | vader en moeder.
Naem Marten gebooren De 16 January gedoopt De 21 february 1779

Ouders | Isack van blercom | getuygen |
Sara Cornnes | | De vader en moeder
Naem Daniel geboren 26 January gedoopt De 21 february 1779

Ouders | Marten Ryerson | getuygen | Johannes Ryerson
vrouwetye van winkel | | Catelyntye Berre
Naem Johannes Geboren De 22 february gedoopt De 21 Mert 1779

Ouders | Jacob gerritse | getuygen | De vader
Eva hellem | | en Moeder
Naem Piter geboren De 21 february gedoopt de 21 Mert 1779

---

*I. e., Demarest, originally and until late years pronounced *Demaray*, the name being French.

Ouders | Jacob Stols | getuygen | Isack kankelen
| henne Miller | | en Zyn vrou
Naem Jannetye gebooren De 12 Decemb 1778 gedoopt De 21 Mert
1779

Ouders | Jacob Spier | getuygen | Cocuraad Vreriese
| Marregriet vreriese* | | Sara husk
Naem Sam gebooren De 5 March gedoopt De 4 April 1779

Ouders | Dirck van Rypen | getuygen | Isack Schuyler
| Elisabeth Meed | | Marregriet Zyn wyf
Naem Marregriet gebooren De 7 March gedoopt De 4 April 1779

Ouders | Jillis Meed | getuygen | Johannes Neefye
| Sara Santvort | | Lena Dy
Naem Willeem gebooren De 8 Mert gedoopt De 11 April 1779

Ouders | hendrick Jacobosse | getuygen | De vader
| Lena Ryerson | | en geunetye Ryerson
Naem Sara gebooren De 20 April gedoopt De 9 May 1779

Ouders | Jacob van Saen | getuygen |
| Ester goetsyest† | | De vader en Moeder
Naem augnietye gebooren De 18 May gedoopt De 20 June 1779

Ouders | Johannes Retau | getuygen | Jacobos Retan
| Sara Spier | | willimye Bogert
Naem Jacobos gebooren De 16 May gedoopt De 20 June 1779

Ouders | Samuel van Saen | getuygen | ari: Westervelt
| Leya Zabrisko | | geertye Zabrisko
Naem Annaetye gebooren De 9 June gedoopt De 4 July 1779

Ouders | Cornelus van winkel | getuygen | Johannes Ackerman
| aunaetye van Rypen | | Castynna Peterse
Naem Johannes gebooren De 26 May gedoopt De 4 July 1779

Ouders | Jacob Doorremus | getuygen | De
| Neeltye pier | | vader en Moeder
Naem Maria gebooren De 9 June gedoopt De 4 July 1779

Ouders | Johannes van gisen | getuygen | De Vader en
| Metye van houten | | Catrienna van honten
Naem Elisabeth gebooren De 9 July gedoopt De 25 July 1779

Ouders | hendrick ackerman | getuygen |
| Marregriet Post | | De vader en Moeder
Naem abraham gebooren De 10 July gedoopt De 22 Agustus 1779

Ouders | Johannes Ryerson | getuygen | Johannes Ryerson
| Elsye Lesier | | Maria Wesselse
Naem Johannes gebooren De 10 July gedoopt De 5 Siptember 1779

Ouders | Nethaneel Kliffin | getuygen | De
| Sara Kint | | vader en Moeder
Naem Maria gebooren De 19 Agustus gedoopt De 19 Siptember 1779

ouders | Cornelus van Derhoof | getuygen | Poulis Ratan
| mareet Cryser | | Jannetye bord
Naem Cornelus gebooren De 18 augustus gedoopt De 3 Siptembre 1779

Ouders | Simon van winkel | getuygen | EDo Merselis
| Antye Merselis | | Arreynente Sip
Naem EDo gebooren De 14 october gedoopt De 31 october 1779

*Frericks.
†Goetschiue.

Onder | Sara Slot | getuygen | De Moeder
Naem Elisabeth fisser geboren De 31 agust gedoopt De 31 october 1779

Onders | Jacob Jacobosse / Sara Jacobosse | getuygen | Jacobos Jacobosse / Neeltye van ness
Naem Jacob geboren De 14 october gedoopt De 31 october 1779

Onders | gerrit gerritse / Marregrietye gerritse | getuygen | De / Vader en Moeder
Naem klasye geboren De 10 November gedoopt De 28 November 1779

onders | Jacob Vreland / geertye van winkel | getuygen | Jacob van winkel / Elsye keep
Naem geerty geboren De 29 November gedoopt 12 December 1779

ouders | hendrick hennion / Maria Romyn | getuygen | Cornelis van houten / Antye hennion
Naem Annetye geboren De 13 December gedoopt De 25 December 1779 CorsDagh*

Ouders | David Doorremus / Leya Provo | getuygen | Cornelis Doorremus / Sara Ryerson
Naem Sara geboren De 12 December 1779 gedoopt De 1 January 1780

Ouders | Petrus van houten / Leya van Rypen | getuygen | Jurre van Rypen / Antye van Rypen
Naem Maregrietye geboren De 15 December 1779 gedoopt De 23 January 1880

Ouders | Hendrick Doorremus / Marregrietye hennion | getuygen | Roelif van houten / Antye hennion
Naem Johannis hinneon geboren De 14 January gedoopt De 6 februar y 1780

Ouders | Roelif van houten / Marregrietye Scherer | getuygen | Cornelis R van houten / Willemyntye van houten
Naem Annaetye geboren De 16 January gedoopt De 20 februar y 1780

Ouders | John van blarcom / Maria Jacobosse | getuygen | Marten v blercom / Maria van Nes
Naem Marritye geboren De 20 January gedoopt De 20 februar y 1780

Ouders | Thomas Cheppel / Maria godwin | getuygen | Jan Cheppel / ginne Cheppel
Naem ginne geboren De 26 February gedoopt De 23 April 1780

Ouders | Jan Banta / Lena bord | getuygen | Dirk Banta / Antye Ratan
Naem Dirk geboren De 17 Mart gedoopt De 23 April 1780

Ouders | hendrick Spier / Maria Drummund | getuygen | EDo Merselis / Arreyaenye Sip
Naem benyamen geboren De 21 februar y gedoopt De 23 April 1780

Ouders | thomas Parcells / Eleonar Parcells | getuygen | John Sandford / Susanna Sandford
Naem Staats geboren De 3 Mart gedoopt De 23 April 1780

onders | Roelif van houten / Antye hennion | getuygen | Johannes Post / Catrienna v: houten
Naem Elisabeth geboren De 22 April gedoopt De 4 June 1780

*I. e., Kersdag, Christmas day.

ouders | gerrit van Derhoef | | getuygen | Johonnes Meed
| Socke Mekerte | | | Marregrietye Demot
Naem Elisabeth gebooren De 5 Agustus gedoopt De 10 September 1780

ouders | Jon Schermhorn | getuygen | De Vader en
| anna Doorte Freriese | | Moeder
Naem Conraed gebooren De 20 November gedoopt De 17 December 1780

Ouders | Salomon Van Debeck | getuygen |
| geesye terhune | | De Vader en Moeder
Naem Ragel gebooren De De 17 December 1780 gedoopt De 21 January 1781

Ouders | Baernt Cool | getuygen | Poulis Ratan
| Catrina van De water | |
Naem Marregriet gebooren De 22 November 1780 gedoopt De 21 January 1781

Ouders | Antoni Van blercom | getuygen | Hendrick Cool
| Annaetye Cook | | Aeltye Post
Naem Hendrick gebooren De 28 January gedoopt De 4 Mert 1781

Ouders | Petrus Doorremus | getuygen | Johannes Neefye
| Maria Dy | | Lena Dij
Naem Jacob gebooren De 14 January gedoopt De 4 Mert 1781

Ouders | Jan van houten | getuygen | Cornelus Van houten
| Lena van houten | | Sara Demarest
Naem Cornelus gebooren De 13 Mert gedoopt D 1 April 1781

Ouders | Philip Dey | getuygen | De
| Janetye Post | | Vader en Moeder
Naem Theunis gebooren De 6 february gedoopt De 15 April 1781

Ouders | Luycas van Saen | getuygen | David berdan
| Lena Berdan | | Castina Roomyn
Naem David gebooren De 20 Mert gedoopt De 15 April 1781

ouders | Nicaso van blercom | getuygen | Hendrick van blercom
| katrina Post | | Annaetye van Winele
Naem vrouwitye gebooren De 25 Mert gedoopt De 15 April 1781

Ouders | Johannis gerritse | getuygen | Simon van Winele
| antye van winkel | | Claesye gerritse
Naem Hendrick gebooren De 28 Mert gedoopt De 15 April 1781

Ouders | henderick Doorremus | getuygen | De vader
| Marregriet van winkel | | en Moeder
Naem hendrick gebooren De 21 Mert gedoopt De 22 April 1781

Ouders | Peter Kinan | getuygen | De Vader
| Mary fiyn | | en Moeder
Naem Mary gebooren De 9 April gedoopt De 6 May 1781

| | | Jan van Rypen
Ouders | Direk van houten | getuygen | Maria Winne
| Maria van Rypen | | Adreyaen van houten
| | | Elisabeth van houten
Naemen De Ene is Maria De Naem Van Die andere is gerritye gebooren De 8 Mart gedoopt De 6 May 1781

Ouders | Joannes WesterVelt | getuygen | Johannis westervelt
| Elisabeth bogert | | Antye bogert
Naem Luycas gebooren De 18 Mert gedoopt De 6 May 1781

6

Ouders | Marten Ryerson / Vrouwitye van winkel | getuygen | Simeon Van winkle / Antye Merselis
Naem Vrouwitye geboooren De 27 Mert gedoopt De 6 May 1781

ouders | Mattheus Van Derhoef / Elisabeth Bennet | getuygen | De / Vader en Moeder
Naem Cornelis gebooren 27 april gedoopt De 20 May 1781

ouders | Joannes Post / Catrina van houten | getuygen | De vader en Moeder en / Cornelus R Van houten
Naem Jannetye gebooren De 20 April Gedoopt De 20 May 1781

ouders | Hessel Ryerson / Doosse Erl | getuygen | Marregriet yeraleMan
Naem Enogh gebooren De 8 April gedoopt De 20 May 1781

ouders | Jacob Spier / Maregriet Vreriese | getuygen | CoenRaed Vreriese / Sara Zy wyf
Naem Coenraed gebooren De 27 April gedoopt De 20 May 1781

ouders | Nicholas kocoro / Peterye van blercom | getuygen | De Vader en Moeder
Naem Arcyaenthe gebooren De 1 May gedoopt De 20 May 1781

ouders | Johannes Hennion / Elisabeth Berre | getuygen | Cornelis Van houten / Antye hennion
Naem gerrit gebooren De 21 April gedoopt De 27 May 1781

ouders | Adreyaen h Van houten / Marritye Codmus | getuygen | Adreyaen g Van houten / Elisabeth Van houten
Naem Elisabeth gebooren De 18 May gedoopt De 4 June 1781 Pinkster

ouders | Adreyaen Post / Sara Spier | getuygen | Johannes Westervelt / Elisabeth Bogert
Naem Petrus gebooren De 30 April gedoopt de 17 June 1781

ouders | Jores Sindel / Hesther Jacobusse | getuygen | Jurien kiesler / Jannetije Jacobusse
Naem Christoffel gebooren De 9 July gedoopt De 13 August 1781

ouders | Johannes van giesen / Metye van honten | getuygen | De vader en Moeder
Naem Marretye gebooren De 16 Agustus gedoopt De 23 September 1781

Ouders | Petrus van houten / Ragel Lerroe | getuygen | De Vader en Moeder
Naem annetye gebooren De 31 January gedoopt De 23 September 1781

ouders | Jan alyo / Elisabeth mandeveel | getuygen | Piter Mandeveel / Miria Bertolf
Naem grietye gebooren De 10 agustus gedoopt De 23 Siptember 1781

Ouders | hindrick Lerroe / Marritye Mandeviel | getuygen | Piter Mandeviel / Maria Bertolf
Naem Maria gedoopt De 7 october gebooren De 2 September 1781

ouders | William Norcros / Eva hennion | getuygen | Johannes hennion / Catlyntye Demod
Naem David gebooren De 21 September gedoopt De 21 october 1781

ouders | Dirck van houten / Ragel neukerk | getuygen. | De Vader en Moeder
Naem Catluntye gebooren De 6 octoober 1781 gedoopt De 4 November

ouders | george L Ryerson | getuygen | De
        | Polly Ryerson | | Vader en Moeder
Naem Joannes gebooren De 23 october gedoopt De 2 December 1781

ouders | george Wilson | getuygen | Jacob Vreland
        | annaetye Vreland | | geertye Van winkel
Naem Sevya geboren De 24 october gedoopt De 2 December 1781

ouders | Johannes Ratan | getuygen | Tuenes Spier
        | Antye Nix | | fiytye Schermhoorn
Naem Sara geboren De 10 November gedoopt De 13 December 1781

ouders | gerret Veder | getuygen | De
        | antye keep | | Vader en moeder
Naem Johannes geboren De 24 october gedoopt De 25 December 1781

ouders | gerrit gerritse | getuygen | De
        | grietye gerritse | | Vader en Moeder
Naem Hendrick geboren De 16 Jannary gedoopt De 3 february 1782

ouders | Jacobus Bertolf | getuygen | De
        | Metye Post | | Vader en Moeder
Naem Gelynem geboren De 25 July 1781 gedoopt De 3 february 1782

Een kint gedoopt de 19 May 1782 omtrent 3 yaer out* De getuygen waren

Naem Elisabeth | Nickolas Demarest
                 Elisabeth Lazier

Ouders | Nicholas Bogert | getuygen | William Strachan
        | Alida Retszema | | Helena Bogert
Naem Nicholas geboren De 23 April gedoopt De 2 June 1782

ouders | Hendrick Jacobosse † | getuygen | Marten van blercom
        | Lena van blercom | | en Zyn Vrou Antye
Naem Elisabeth geboren De 18 May gedoopt De 16 June 1782

ouders | Cillip hael† | getuygen | David Doorremus
        | ketrienna Boss | | Leya Provo
Naem ketriena geboren De 16 october 1781 gedoopt De 30 June 1782

ouders | Tomas Cheppel | getuygen | Abraham van Derbeek
        | Maria godwin | | Marregriet godwin
Naem abraham geboren De   gedoopt De 14 July 1782

ouders | Tomas Parcells | getuygen | De Vader
        | Elenor Parcells | | en Elisabeth Post
Naem Samuel geboren De 10: April gedoopt de 14: July 1782

ouders | Simion van winkel | getuygen | Martin Ryerson
        | Antye Merselis | | Vrouwetye van winkel
Naem Piter geboren De 27 June gedoopt De 28 July 1782

ouders | Roelif van houten | getuygen | De
        | Aeltye Doorremus | | Vader en Moeder
Naem Roelif geboren De 3 agustus gedoopt De 25 agustus 1782

July De 26 is geboren Een kint van geertruy Van houten en is gedoopt De
25 augustus en is genaemt Joannes Van houten 1782
De getuygen feytye van houten

*A child baptized about three years old. No parent's name is given. It may have
been adopted about this time.
†Query: Caleb Hall?

ouders | Johannes gerritse / antye van winkel | getuygen | Abraham van winkel / Sara Van winkel
Naem Elisabeth gebooren De 24 Siptember gedoopt De 20 October 1782

ouders | Daniel Vandel / annaetye van houten | getuygen | De / Vader en Moeder
Naem Maria gebooren De 6 September 1781 gedoopt De 3 November 1782

ouders | Adreyaen van houten / Elisabeth van houten | getuygen | gerrebrant van houten en De / Moeder van het kint
Naem Adreyaen gebooren De 1 November gedoopt De 17 November 1782

Ouders | Philip Dey / Jannetye Post | getuygen | De / Vader en Moeder
Naem Catlyntye gebooren De 14: November gedoopt De 1 December 1782

ouders | Jan T van blercom / Maria Jacobosse | getuygen | Johannes Ryerson / Elsye Lazier
Naem Johannes gebooren De 27 November gedoopt De 25 December 1782

Ouders | Dirk Dey / henne Pierson | getuygen | Tuenes Dey en / hester Schuyler
Naem tuenes gebooren De 17 January 1777 gedoopt in De gemeente van Totowa

ouders | Dirk Dey / henne Pierson | getuygen | Philip Dey / en hester Dey
Naem Maria gebooren De 20 Agustus 1778 gedoopt in De gemeente van totowa

ouders | Dirk Dey / henne Pierson | getuygen | De Vader / en Moeder
Naem Pierson gebooren De 8 Mert 1780 gedoopt in De gemeente Van Totowa

Ouders | Dirk Dey / henne Pierson | getuygen | De / Vader en moeder
Naemen De Eennen Nence De andere Elisabeth gebooren De 11 July 1782 gedoopt in De gemeente Van Totowa

ouders | Marten van blercom / Antye van Veght | getuygen | Hendrick Jacobosse
Naem Marretye gebooren De 23 November gedoopt De 25 December 1782

Ouders | Dirck Van houten / Maria Van Rypen | getuygen | De Vader en Moeder
Naem adreyaen gebooren De 7 December gedoopt De 25 December 1782

Ouders | Cornelis Van Rypen / Marretye gerritse | getuygen | frans post / Marregriet Van Rypen
Naem Johannes gebooren De 23 October 1782 gedoopt De 5 January 1783

Ouders | Johannes Meed / Maregriet Demod | getuygen | Jacob Demod / Antye Demod
Naem Jores gebooren De 13 December 1782 gedoopt De 19 January 1783

Ouders | gerrit yacoborse | Comfort kreen* | getuygen | De Vader en Moeder
Naem yannetye gebooren De 11 Jannarij gedoopt De 2 february 1783

Ouders | Hendrick Spier | Maria Drummund | getuygen | Derck Van Rypen | Elisabeth Meed
Naem Dirck gebooren De 21 December 1782 gedoopt De 2 february 1783

ouders | Jacob Vreland | geertyc Van winkel | getuygen | De Vader en Moeder
Naem Jacob gebooren De 22 february gedoopt De 30 Mert 1783

Ouders | Enogh Vreland | Jennicke Merselis | getuygen | Edo Merselis | Arreyacnthe Sip
Naem Edo gebooren De 16 Mert gedoopt De 13 april 1783

Ouders | Sollomon Woldron | Elisabeth gorden | getuygen | Adolf Waldron | Catrienna fienixt
Naem Catrina gebooren De 9 Mert gedoopt De 13 April 1783

ouders | Bornt Cool | Cornelia Van De water | getuygen | De Vader en Moeder
Naem gerrit gebooren De 14 Mert gedoopt De 21 april 1783

ouders | karl Dibevoos | Maria Van houten | getuygen | De Vader en Moeder
Naem Roelif gebooren De 13 April gedoopt De 4 May 1783

ouders | Johannes Post | Antye Ratan | getuygen | Jacob Van winkel | Altye Post
Naem Johannes gebooren De 7 April gedoopt De 18 May 1783

Ouders | Samuel Borbans | Maregriet Yeralemon | getuygen | De Vader en Moeder
Naem Johennes Yeralemon gebooren De 7 April gedoopt De 18 May 1783

ouders | hendrick Boss | annicke Doorremus | getuygen | ari Boss | Cyntye Dooremus
Naem Cyntye gebooren De 24 May gedoopt De 15 June 1763

onders | Johannes hennion | Catelyntye Demot | getuygen | De Vader en Moeder
Naem Jannetye gebooren De 24 May gedoopt De 22 June 1783

onders | Johannes Ratan | Elisabeth Leck | getuygen | Johannes hennion | Catlyntye Demod
Naem Maria gebooren De 1 agustus gedoopt De 17 agustus 1783

ouders | Nickasi Van blercom | Catrina Post | getuygen | Jurre Van Rypen | Zyn Moeder Marregriet
Naem Nickasi gebooren de 16 agustus gedoopt de 31 agustus 1783

ouders | Jan Westervelt | Antye Van Rypen | getuygen | Peter Van houten | Leya Van Rypen
Naem Elisabeth gebooren De 8 September gedoopt De 21 Siptember 1783

ouders · | gerrit Post | Metyntye Bertolf | getuygen |
Naem Marretye gebooren De 27 September gedoopt De 26 october 1783

---

*Crane.
†Phœnix.

ouders | Cornelis hennion / Arreyaentye Veder | getuygen | Johannes hennion / Catlyntye Demod
Naem David geboren De 6 November gedoopt De 7 December 1783

ouders | Dirk Van giesen / Yannetye Van houten | getuygen | Johannes Vangieson / Metye Van houten
Naem Metye geboren De 22 November gedoopt De 21 December 1783

ouders | gerrit Veder / Antye kip | getuygen | Nicase kip / Leya Mandeviel
Naem Nicase geboren De 25 December 1783 gedoopt De 25 January 1784

ouders | Cornelus Van houten / feytye Van houten | getuygen | Hessel Pieterse / feytye Van houten
Naem Robbert geboren De 3 January gedoopt De 15 february 1784

ouders | Roelif Van houten / Aeltye Doorremis | getuygen | De Vader en Moeder
Naem hendrick geboren De 21 January gedoopt De 15 february

Ouders | Dirck Van houten / Maria Van Rypen | getuygen | Johannes Van winkel / gerritye Sip
Naem Adreyaen geboren De 2 Mert gedoopt De 21 Mert 1784

ouders | Jacob Spier / grietye Vreriese | getuygen | De Vader en Moeder
Naem annaetye geboren De 16 Mert gedoopt De 11 April 1784

ouders | Piter gerritse / EVa Romyn | getuygen | De Vader en Moeder
Naem antye geboren De 13 Mert gedoopt De 11 April 1784

Ouders | Johannes Berdan / Jannetye Ryerson | getuygen | Johannes Ryerson / Elisabeth yeraelman
Naem Dirk geboren De 29 february gedoopt De 11 April 1784

ouders | Dirk Van houten / Ragel Post | getuygen | De Vader en Moeder
Naem Mertijnes geboren De 11 Mert gedoopt De 25 april 1784

ouders | Jacob Doorremus / Neeltye Pier | getuygen | De Vader en Moeder
Naem Elisabeth geboren De 6 Mert gedoopt De 25 april 1784

ouders | hessel Ryerson / Docie Erl | getuygen | Piter Van aellen / Maria hopper
Naem Piter geboren De 20 Mert gedoopt De 9 May 1784

ouders | hendrick Jacobosse / Sara Sisko | getuygen | De Vader en Moeder
Naem Marritye geboren De 5 May gedoopt De 20 1784 June

ouders | Jan Ryerson / Elsye Lazier | getuygen | De Vader en Moeder
Naem Polle geboren De 6 June gedoopt De 20 June 1784

ouders | adreyaen P Post / Sara Spier | getuygen | Johannes Spier / altye Spier
Naem Johannes geboren De 13 June gedoopt De 11 July 1784

ouders | Thunes Spier / feytye Schermhoorn | getuygen | De Vader en Moeder
Naem Jacob geboren De 14 June gedoopt De 11 July 1784

ouders | Roelif Van houten | getuygen | Johannes Van houten
Catrijna Van houten | | Loybethe Van Rypen
Naem Johannes gebooren De 13 July 1784   gedoopt De 1 Agustus 1784

ouders | Phelip Dey | getuygen | De
Jannetye Post | | Vader en Moeder
Naem Nency gebooren De 21 Augustus gedoopt De 26 September 1784

Ouders | hendrick Jacobosse | getuygen | De Vader en Moeder
Lena Van blercom | | en antone Van blercom
Naem geertery gebooren De 9 Augustus gedoopt De 26 September 1784

Ouders | William Norcross | getuygen | aroudt Scuylder
Eva hennion | |
Naem william gebooren De 20 June gedoopt De 10 october 1784

Ouders | hendrick keerte | getuygen | Jellis Van Ness
Leya Mandeviel | | trynye Mandeveel
Naem Suzanna gebooren De 26 September gedoopt 17 october 1784

ouders | gerret Jacobosse | getuygen | De
Comfort kreen | | Vader en Moeder
Naem annetye gebooren De 4 November gedoopt De 5 December 1784

ouders | Bornt kool | getuygen | David godwin
Cornelia Van De water | |
Naem Bornt gebooren De 5 November gedoopt De 5 December 1784

ouders | antoni Van blercom | getuygen | adreyaen kool
anaetye kool | | Elisabeth Lutye
Naem Vrouwetye gebooren De 6 November gedoopt De 5 December 1784

ouders | Jacob Van winkel | getuygen | Helmigh Van giese
Catelyntye neeffe | | Marritye Neeffe
Naem Jacob gebooren De 21 November gedoopt De 25 December 1784

Ouders | adreyaen Van houten | getuygen | Johannes Van winkel
Marretye Codmos | | gerritye Sip
Naem adreyaen gebooren De 13 December 1784 gedoopt De 2 January 1785

ouders | Piter Remse | getuygen | Jacob berdan
yannetye Ryerson | | Rebecke Ryerson
Naem Piter gebooren De 11 January gedoopt De 6 februari 1785

ouders | Simion Van winkel | getuygen | Corneles Merselis
antye Merselis | | Marritye Neeffe
Naem Cornelis gebooren De 13 January gedoopt De 6 february 1785

onders | thunis Ryerson | getuygen | De
Marritye Ryerson | | Vader en Moeder
Naem abraham gebooren De 25 Jaunary gedoopt De 20 february 1785

ouders | tomas Doorremus | getuygen | Johannes Doorremus
Ragel Spier | | Sara Mandeviel
Naem Johaunes gebooren De 17 January gedoopt De 20 february 1785

ouders | Roelif Van houten | getuygen | Cornelis Van houten
antye Berdan | | feytye Van houten
Naem antye gebooren De 17 february gedoopt De 13 Mart 1785

Ouders | Dirck Van houten | getuygen | De
Ragel Post | | Vader en Moeder
Naem Dirck gebooren De 27 May gedoopt De 12 June 1785

Ouders | Piter Van houten | getuygen | De
Leya Van Rypen | | Vader & Moeder
Naem Hellemigh　geboooren De 10 July　gedoopt De 24 July 1785

ouders | Samuel Borhans | getuygen | De
Marregrietye yeraleman | | Vader en Moeder
Naem Catrina　geboooren De 26 June　gedoopt De 24 July 1785

ouders | Cornelus heunion | getuygen | David heunion
arreyaentye Veder | | antye kep wedevrou*
Naem gerrit　geboooren De 23 augustus　gedoopt De 18 September 1785

ouders | Johannes Ratan | getuygen | De
Elisabeth Leeckt† | | Vader en Moeder
Naem Neeltye　geboooren De 12 Agustus　gedoopt De 2 october 1785

ouders | hendrick Ratan | getuygen | Johannes Ratan
antye Lint | | antye nuks
Naem Sara　geboooren De 6 July　gedoopt De 23 october 1785

ouders | Roelif Van houten | getuygen | De
aeltye Doorremus | | Vader en Moeder
Naem Sara　geboooren De 4 october　gedoopt De 13 November 1785

Ouders | Jores Doorremus | getuygen | Aegge Doorremus
Jannetye Ryerson | |
Naem Henderick　geboooren De 20 November　gedoopt De 18 December
1785

Ouders | Jacob Doorremus · | getuygen | De
Jacomyntye Van houten | | Vader en Moeder
Naem Piter　geboooren De 17 November　gedoopt De 18 December 1785

ouders | John Dey | getuygen | De
Phebe Crain | | Vader en Moeder
Naem John ogdon　geboooren De 6 october 1785　gedoopt De 1 January
1786

onders | gerrit Van Derheof | getuygen | Jacobos Jacobosse
Soeke Mekerte | | Maria Sisko
Naem Maria　geboooren De 6 agustus 1781

ouders | Corneleus Law | getuygen | Dirck Van houten
Catrina toersse* | | Maria Van Rypen
Naem Maria　geboooren De 22 January　gedoopt De 12 Mert 1786

*Tuers.

ouders | Cornelus Van houten | getuygen | Edo Merselis
feytye Van houten | | Lena Van houten
Naem Cornelus　geboooren De 17 february　gedoopt De 12 Mert 1786

Ouders | Renier Berdan | getuygen | Jores Ryerson
antye Ryerson | | francyn Boskerk
Naem antye　geboooren De 23 april　gedoopt De 21 May 1786

Ouders | adman kingsland | getuygen | Piter Dey
ann Low | | Lena Boerd
Naem Piter　geboooren De 23 february　gedoopt De 21 May 1786

Ouders | Jan Ryerson | getuygen | Cornelus lazier
Elsye Lazier | | yannetye ackerman
Naem yannetye　geboooren De 2 May　gedoopt De 4 June 1786

*Widow.
†Lake.

ouders | Jacobos Jacobosse | getuygen | geliaem Demarest
Catriena Demarest | | Zusanna Ratan
Naem Zusanna gebooren De   May   gedoopt De 4 June 1786

Ouder | Marres ackerman | getuygen | Cornelus kip
Elisabeth Lambart | | Cestina Demarest
Naem Johannes gebooren De 5 May   gedoopt De 4 June 1786

Ouders | Jacob gerritse | getuygen | Cornelya banta
Eva hellem |
Naem Cristian gebooren De 9 february   gedoopt op Totowa 1786

Ouders | Philip Dey | getuygen | De
yannetye Post | | Vader en moeder
Naem frans Post gebooren De 2 June   gedoopt De 2 July 1786

Ouders | Cornelus westervelt | getuygen | Yurre westervelt
Maria Robbelin | | Marretye gerritse
Naem antye gebooren De 12 June   gedoopt De 2 July 1786

Ouders | hendrick Van Blercom | getuygen | De
Elisabeth Goetsyes | | Vader en Moeder
Naem annaetye gebooren De 1 July   gedoopt 23 July 1786

Ouders | Johannes Gerritse | getuygen | De
antye Van Winkel | | Vader en Moeder
Naem Lena gebooren De 10 July   gedoopt De 27 agustus 1786

Ouders | audries kebel* | getuygen | Roelif VanDerbeck
antye Van houten | | Doorte kebel
Naem Doorte gebooren De 10 May   gedoopt De 27 agustus 1786

onders | Jacob Doorremus | getuygen | De Vader en moeder
Neeltye Pier |
Naem Cornelis gebooren De 26 July   gedoopt De 27 agustus 1786

onders | Peter gerritse | getuygen | Hendrick hennion
Eva Romine | | Maria Romine
Naem Maria gebooren De 1 Siptember   gedoopt De 1 october 1786

Ouders | Jacob Spier | getuygen | De
Marregriet frerexse | | Vader en moeder
‹ Naem Jacob gebooren De 22 September   gedoopt De 22 october 1786

Ouders | Hendrick Kip | getuygen | Nickase Kip
Catrynna Doorremus | | Leya Mandeveel
Naem Leya gebooren De 29 october   gedoopt De 12 November 1786

Ouders | Samuel Van Saen | getuygen | Cornelus kip
Leya Zabriski | | Kestina Demarest
Naem Ragel gebooren De 6 November   gedoopt 26 Novemr 1786

Ouders | Adreyaen Cool | getuygen | antone Van blercom
Elisabeth Lutsken | | annaetye Cool
Naem annaetye gebooren De 8 November   gedoopt De 17 December 1786

Ouders | Poules Ratan | getuygen | De Vader en Moeder
Metye Spier |
Naem Johannes gebooren De 21 November   gedoopt De 17 December 1786

*Cable
7

Ouders | Hendrick Cool | getuygen | Baernt Cool
abigel Mc kerte* | | Corneleya Van De Water
    Naem Catrina gebooren De 12 November gedoopt De 17 December
1786

Ouders | Johannes Post | getuygen | De
antye Ratan | | Vader en Moeder
    Naem yannetye gebooren De 6 November gedoopt De 17 December
1786

Ouders | Mathew Cranck | getuygen | Helmigh V houten
geertruy Van houten | | feytye Van houten
    Naem Elisabeth gebooren De 14 November gedoopt De 26 December
1786

Ouders | John Dey | getuygen | De
Phebe Green | | Vader en Moeder
    Naem theunes gebooren De 26 November gedoopt De 26 December
1786

ouders | Edo Merselus | getuygen | De Vader en Moeder
Lena Van houten | |
    Naem Marretye gebooren De 6 January gedoopt 11 february 1787

Ouders | Jan Van Debergh | getuygen | Benyamem Delemetter
Antye Deleraetter† | | Claertye Van houten
    Naem Catelyntye gebooren De 14 January gedoopt de 11 february
1787

Ouders | Cornelus Van houten | getuygen | De
Metye Van houten | | Vader en Moeder
    Naem Jannetye gebooren De 29 January gedoopt De 25 february 1787

Ouders | Roelif Van houten | getuygen | De
Aeltye Doorremus | | Vader en Moeder
    Naem Jacob gebooren De 21 february gedoopt de 18 March 1787

Ouders | Hendrick Doorremus | getuygen | De Vader
Marregriet hennion | | en Moeder
    Naem Hessel gebooren De 19 february gedoopt De 18 March 1787

Ouders | Dirrick Degray | getuygen | De Vader
Annaetye Schuyler | | en Moeder
    Naem Jan geboren De 10 february gedoopt De 18 March 1787

Ouders | Adreyaen Van houten | getuygen | De
Marretye Codmus | | Vader en Moeder
    Naem Dirck gebooren De 1 May 1787 gedoopt De 20 May 1787

Ouders | Derck Dey | getuygen | De
hannah Pearson | | Vader en moeder
    Naem Hester gebooren 9 october 1784 gedoopt op Hackensack By
Domine Romyn

Ouders | Derck Dey | getuygen | Do
hannah Pearson | | Vader en Moeder
    Naem Jane gebooren De 11 March gedoopt De 20 May 1787

Ouders | Dirk Van giesen | getuygen | De
yannetye Van houten | | Vader en Moeder
    Naem Leybetye gebooren De 29 May gedoopt De 17 June 1787

*Abigail McCarty.
†Evidently erroneously copied from a memorandum of the name De La Mater.

Ouders | Johannes hennion | getuygen | Johannes Van houten
Elisabeth Berri | | Maria Berri
Naem Maria geboorcn D 27 May gedoopt De 8 July 1787

Ouders | David Doorremus | getuygen | De
Elisabeth Van houten | | Vader en Moeder
Naem Maria geboorcn De 4 Juno gedoopt De 8 July 1787

Ouders | Cornelus Van Winkel | getuygen | Dirk Stentcn
Annathe Van Rypen | | Jinne Ryerson
Naem Jaunetye geboorcn De 12 Augustus gedoopt De 16 September 1787

Ouders | gerrit gerritse | getuygen | Do vader
Marregriet gerritse | | en Moeder
Naem Lena geboorcn De 11 Augustus gedoopt De 16 September 1787

Ouders | Roelif R Van houten | getuygen | De
Antye Berdan | | Vader en Moeder
Naem Marregrietye geboorcn De 1 October gedoopt de 28 October 1787

Ouders | Johannes Berdan | getuygen | Do
Jaunetye Ryerson | | Vader en Marregriet Berdan
Naem Marregrietye geboorcn De 9 September gedoopt De 28 October 1787

Ouders | Hendrick Jacobosse | getuygen | De
Lena Van Blercom | | Vader en Moeder
Naem Antoni geboorcn 8 october gedoopt De 8 November 1787

Ouders | Johannes Westervelt | getuygen | Hans Post
Leya Provost | | en Zyn huysvrou
Naem David geboorcn De 5 December gedoopt De 30 Decembr 1787

Ouders | Johannes Ryerson | getuygen | De
Elsye Lazier | | Vader en Moeder
Naem Maria geboorcn 9 December gedoopt De 30 December 1787

Ouders | Piter Mersalus | getuygen | Edo Mersalus
yaunetye Van winkel | | arreyacntye Sep
Naem Edo geboorcn De 20 December gedoopt De 13 January 1788

Ouders | Adreyaen Post | getuygen | Abram Bogert
Maria Spear | | Antye gerretse
Naem Antye geboorcn De 4 December gedoopt De 13 January 1788

Ouders | Johannes Post | getuygen | Daniel SchoonMaker
Catrina Van houten | | en Maria Post
Naem Johannes geboorcn De 8 January gedoopt De 3 february 1788

Ouders | Anthoni Van Blercom | getuygen | Johannes Post
Annaetye Cook | | Antye Rutan
Naem Annaetye geboorcn De 27 Decemr 1787 gedoopt De 3 february 1788

Ouders | David hennion | getuygen | Hendrick Doorremus
Antye kep | | Marregriet hennion
Naem Hendrick geboorcn De 6 february gedoopt De 9 March 1788

Ouders | Benyamen Delemerter | getuygen | yannetye Van houten
klaertye Van houten | |
Naem yannetye geboorcn De 30 January gedoopt De 9 March 1788

Ouders | Samuel Borhans | getuygen | De
Marregriet Jeralemau | | Vader en Moeder
Naem Samuel geboren De 17 January gedoopt de 24 Mert 1788

Ouders | keryncs Bertolf | getuygen | Petrus Van Alen
Susanna Van Alen | | | Maria hopper
Naem Johannes   geboren De 12 april   gedoopt De 11 May 1788

onders | Johannes fr post | getuygen | De
Marretye Neeffe | | | Vader en Moeder.
Naem francoos   Geboren De 12 May   gedoopt De 8 June 1788

Ouders | Andries Cable | getuygen | Jannetye Ryerson
Antye Van houten | | | wife Van Dirck Stenton
Naem Antye   gebooren De   gedoopt De 6 July 1788

Ouders | gerrit Neeffe | getuygen | Hendreck hennion
Eva Van honten | | | Maria Romyn
Naem Roelef   gebooren De 23 June   gedoopt De 20 July 1788

Ouders | Philip Dey | getuygen | De
Jannetye Post | | | Vader en Moeder
Naem Johannes   gebooren De 23 June   gedoopt De 20 July 1788

Ouders | Poulis Ratan | getuygen | De
Metye Spier | | | Vader en Moeder
Naem Jannetye   gebooren De 21 June 1788   gedoopt De 17 Agustus

Ouders | Dirck Van houten | getuygen | Abraham Van Rypen
Maria Van Rypen | | | Neesye gerritse
Naem Neesye   gebooren De 4 Agustus 1788   gedoopt De 17 Agustus 1788

Ouders | William Santvort | getuygen | De
Maria Van Ness | | | Vader en Moeder
Naem Johannes   gebooren De 18 Agustus   gedoopt De 14 September 1788

Ouders | Nicase Van blercom | getuygen | Jan van blercom
katrienna post | | | Antye Jacobosse
Naem Leua   gebooren De 19 September   gedoopt De 26 october 1788

Ouders | Jacob Doorremus | getuygen | De
Neeltye Pier | | | Vader en Moeder
Naem Susanna   gebooren De   gedoopt De 26 october 1788

Ouders | Are Meed | getuygen | Johannes Meed
Sara Jacobosse | | | en Zyn Vron
Naem Elisabeth   gebooren De 27 September   gedoopt De 9 November
1788

Ouders | Johannes Van gieson | getuygen | De Vader en Moeder en
Metye Van houten | | | Adreyaen Van houten en
Twelingen | | | Marretye Cadmos
Naemmen Cornelus en Adreyaen   gebooren De 7 October   gedoopt De 9
November 1788

Ouders | Johannes post | getuygen | De
Antye Rattau | | | Vader en Moeder
Naem francoos   gebooren De 12 october   gedoopt De 9 November 1788

Ouders | Abraham Van Rypen | getuygen | De
Aeltye Post | | | vader en Moeder
Naem Ragel   gebooren De 16 of* 17 october   gedoopt De 23 November
1788

Ouders | Hendrick Jacobosse | getuygen | De Vader en Moeder
Sara Sisko | | |
Naem Johannes   gebooren De 29 September 1788   gedoopt De 18 January 1789

*Of in Holland means or. "The 16th or 17th of October.

Ouders | Tomas Doorremus / Elisabeth Van houten | getuygen | De / Vader en Moeder
    Naem Marretye gebooren De 10 December 1788 gedoopt De 18 January 1789

Ouders | Dirck Van houten / Ragel Post | getuygen | De / Vader en Moeder
    Naem Lybetye geboren De 30 December 1788 gedoopt De 1 february 1789

Ouders | Jurre Van Rypen / Maria Berdan | getuygen | Jacob Berdan / Rebecka Ryerson
    Naem Jacob geboore De 3 January 1789 gedoopt De 1 february 1789

Ouders | Piter Dey / Lena Board | getuygen | De / Vader en Moeder
    Naem Maria geboore De 12 December 1788 gedoopt De 1 february 1789

ouders | Piter Dey / Lena Board | getuygen | De / Vader en Moeder
    Naem Johanna geboore De 12 June gedoopt De 23 July 1787

ouders | Isack Van ness / Merce Conselver | getuygen | De / Vader en Moeder
    Naem Annaetye geboore De 6 December 1788 gedoopt De 15 february 1789

Ouders | Hendrick kepp / Catrina Doorremus | getuygen | David I hennion / Antye kepp
    Naem Marretye geboore De 26 January 1788 gedoopt De 15 february 1789

Ouders | Adreyaen Van houten / yannetye Roomyn | getuygen | De / Vader en Moeder
    Naem Piter geboore De 31 January gedoopt D 1 Marth 1789

Ouders | Jacobos Jacobosse / Dinne kestede | getuygen | Sendel / Marregriet Jacobosse
    Naem Sara geboore De 26 february gedoopt De 29 March 1789

Ouders | Pryntye Van wenkel* | getuygen | De Moeder
    Naem Abram post geboore De 11 Mart gedoopt De 24 May 1789

Ouders | Isaack pier / Maria Post | getuygen | De / Vader en Moeder
    Naem Johannes geboore De 11 April gedoopt De 24 May 1789

Ouders | Joseph ketchanon / Bronn | getuygen | De / Vader en Moeder
    Naem Jeams geboore De 26 January gedoopt De 24 May 1789

ouders | gerrit Jacobosse / Comfort kreen | getuygen | De / Vader en Moeder
    Naem Sara geboore De 21 April gedoopt De 24 May 1789

ouders | Johannes Banta / Jannety Van Syl | getuygen | Jan Romyn / Leentye Stagg
    Naem Cetrina geboore De 22 July gedoopt D 23 Agustus 1789

*See page 64.

Ouders | Johannes Post | getuygen | David van blercom
| Elisabeth ackerman | | Maria Zyn Vrou
Naem Metye gebooren De 6 Agustus gedoopt De 23 Augustus 1789

Ouders | John van blarcom | getuygen | De Vader
| Maria Jacobosse | | en Moeder
Naem Anthoni gebooren De 11 Agustus gedoopt De 6 September 1789

Ouders | Direk freland | getuygen | De vader
| Maria fiser | | en Moeder
Namen Elisabeth en Maria gebooren D   gedoopt De 6 September 1789

Ouders | John Styls | getuygen | De Vader en
| Mary Sandford | | Moeder
Naem Saley gebooren De July 26 gedoopt De 6 September 1789

Ouders | Hendrick Merceker | getuygen | De vader
| Maria kranck | | en Moeder
Naem Abraham gebooren De 15 July gedoopt De 6 September 1789

Ouders | Gelyn ackerman | getuygen | Dircke ackerman
| trynye Mandeviel | |
Naem hendrick gebooren De 17 Agustus gedoopt De 4 October 1789

Ouders | Roelif Van houten | getuygen | De
| Antye Berdan | | Vader en Moeder
Naem Adreyaen gebooren De 10 September gedoopt De 4 october 1789

ouders | Roelif H Van houten | getuygen | Johannes Van
| Catriyna Van houten | | giesen Metye Van houten
Naem helmigh gebooren De 9 September gedoopt De 4 october 1789

Ouders | Johannes Storm | getuygen | De Vader en
| Maria Willis | | Moeder
Naem Ragel gebooren De 3 September gedoopt De 4 October 1789

Ouders | Abraham gerritse | getuygen | De Vader en
| yannetye hennion | | Moeder
Naem Maria gebooren De 3 September gedoopt De 4 october 1789

ouders | Jan handkock | getuygen | De
| Jenne Van blercom | | Vader en Moeder
Naem Authoni gebooren 13 September gedoopt De 18 October 1789

Ouders | Samuel Borhaus | getuygen | De
| Morregrietye Jeraleman | | Vader en Moeder
Naem Jacobos gebooren De 25 September gedoopt De 18 October 1789

Ouders | Adreyaen Post | getuygen | frans Spier en Zyn
| Maria Spier | | huysvrou
Naem grietye gebooren 26 September gedoopt De 18 October 1789

Ouders | Mathens kranck | getuygen | Egge Doorremus
| geertruy Van houten | |
Naem John gebooren De 6 october 1789 gedoopt D 1 November 1789

Ouders | Hessel hennion | getnygen | David Brower
| Catryn Brower | | Arreyaenthe Stymets
Naem Arreyaente gebooren De 11 October gedoopt De 1 September 1789

onders | Hessel Ryerson | getuygen | De
| Catrien Van Veghter | | Vader en Moeder
Naem Dooce gebooren De 9 october gedoopt De 30 November 1789

ouders | David hennion | getuygen | De
| Vrouwetye hennion | | Vader en Moeder •
Naem Myntye gebooren De 29 November 1789 gedoopt De 1 January 1790

Ouders | David D ackerman | getuygen | Jan Ackerman
| Metye Erustues | | Annaetye Brower
Naem Annaetye gebooren De 10 December 1789 gedoopt De 10 Janunary 1790

Ouders | Adreyaen Van houten | getuygen | De Vader en Moeder
| Marretye Codmos |
Naem Cattelyntye gebooren De 29 December 1789 gedoopt De 24 Janary 1790

Ouders | Johaunes Benson | getuygen | Jananues* Benson
| Maria Westervelt | | Jannetye Banta
Naem Jacob gebooren De 21 January gedoopt De 7 february 1790

Ouders | Hendrick Jacobosse | getuygen | Roelif Van houten
| Lena Van blereom | | Antye Berdan
Naem Antye gebooren De 8 January gedoopt De 7 february 1790

ouders | David Dey | getuygen | De Vader en Moeder
| Sara Neeffe |
Naem Hester gebooren De 11 December 1789 gedoopt De 21 March 1790

ouders | frans Ryerson | getuygen | De Vader en Moeder
| yannetye lambert |
Naem Direk gebooren De 2 february gedoopt De 21 March 1790

Ouders | Hendrick Van aellen | getuygen | Petrus Van aellen
| yannetye Lazier | | Maria hopper
Naem yannetye gebooren De 14 february gedoopt De 21 March 1790

Ouders | Cornelus Van houten | getuygen | Roelif Van houten
| feytye Van houten | | Antye Borden
Naem Elisabeth gebooren De 26 february gedoopt de 21 March 1790

ouders | Cornelus Van winkel | getuygen | John ackerman
| Annaetye Van Rypen | | Elsye Boskerk
Naem Yannetye gebooren De 21 february gedoopt De 4 April 1790

Ouders | David Davidse | getuygen | Helmigh Mereeker
| Leya Mereeker | | feytye Ryker
Naem feytye gebooren De 20 february gedoopt De 4 April 1790

Ouders | Helmigh Mereeker | | David Davidse
| feytye Ryker | | Leya Mereeker
Naem Harme gebooren De 23 October gedoopt De 4 April 1790

Ouders | Benyamen Delemeter | getuygen | De Vader en Moeder
| Claentye Van houten |
Naem Catlyntye gebooren De 21 february gedoopt De 4 April 1790

Ouders | Direk Ryerson | getuygen | De
| geesye hopper | | Vader en Moeder
Naem Marretye gebooren De 1 Dagh April gedoopt De 25 April 1790

Ouders | Jan Maar | getuygen | Hendrick koorte
| | Leya Maudeviel
Naem Ruthye gebooren De   Gedoopt De 25 April 1790

*Doubtless a clerical error for Johannes, John.

ouders | Jan Ryerson / Elsye Lazier | getuygen | De / Vader en Moeder
Naem Cornelus   gebooren De 16 April   gedoopt De 9 May 1790

Ouders | John Earl / Ragel ackerman | getuygen | Abraham ackerman / Sara ackerman
Naem Morres   gebooren De 31 March   gedoopt De 9 May 1790

ouders | Thunis hennion / Catrina Kipp | getuygen | De / Vader en Moeder
Naem Johannes   gebooren De 3 May   gedoopt De 24 May 1790

Ouders | Johannes Toers / Lybe Ratan | getuygen | Poulis Ratan / Jannetye Bord
Naem Jannetye   gebooren De 30 April   gedoopt De 24 May 1790

Ouders | Daniel Schoenmaker / Elisabeth Post | getuygen | De / Vader en Moeder
Naem Selli   gebooren De 1 May   gedoopt De 6 June 1790

ouders | Ponles Ratan / Metye Spier | getnygen | De Vader en Moeder
Naem Johannes   gebooren De 19 May   gedoopt De 20 June 1790

ouders | Abraham Ryerson / Sara Mandeviel | getuygen | Jannetye Joans / en De Vader
Naem Nikcoles   gebooren De 14 May   gedoopt De 20 June 1790

Ouders | Jan Merceker / Elisabeth Ryker | getuygen | Helmigh merceker / fyty Ryker
Naem Elias   gebooren De 5 Mert   gedoopt De 4 July 1790

ouders | Ari Meed / Sara Jacobosse | getuygen | De / Vader en Moeder
Naem Adreyaen   gebooren De 17 June   gedoopt De 18 July 1790

ouders | David hennion / Autye kipp | getuygen | De / Vader en Moeder
Naem gerrit   gebooren De 4 July   gedoopt De 1 Agustus 1790

Ouders | Derek van houten / Ragel Post | getuygen | De / Vader en Moeder
Naem adreyaen   gebooren De 26 June   gedoopt De 1 Agustus 1790

onders | Jacobos McColli / Ragel Ackerman | getuygen | De / Vader en Moeder
Naem Abigel   gebooren De 11 June   gedoopt De 1 Agustus 1790

ouders | Derek Degra / Annaetye Schyler | getuygen | De / Vader en Moeder
Naem Rebecke   gebooren De 26 July   gedoopt De 26 September 1790

Ouders | adman kingland / ann low | getuygen | De / Vader en Moeder
Naem Marregrietye   gebooren De 6 June   gedoopt De 24 october 1790

Ouders | Philip Dey / Jannetye Post | getuygen | De / Vader en Moeder
Naem Benyamen   gebooren De 22 Agust   gedoopt De 24 october 1790

ouders | Cornelus Merselis / Maria Post | getuygen | De / Vader en Moeder
Naem Arrinentye   gebooren De 16 October   gedoopt De 7 November 1790

Ouders | gerrit Neeffe | getuygen | De
Catlyntye Post | | Vader en Moeder
Naem Catlyntye gebooren De 3 September gedoopt De 7 November 1790

ouders | Abraham Willis | getuygen | De
Catrina Post | | Vader en Moeder
Naem Catrina gebooren De 17 october gedoopt De 21 November 1790

Ouders | Adreyaen Cool | getuygen | De Vader
Elisabeth Lutskens | | en Moeder
Naem gerret gebooren De 29 october gedoopt De 21 November 1790

Ouders | Edo Merselis | getuygen | De
Lena Van houten | | Vader en Moeder
Naem Edo gebooren De 31 October gedoopt De 21 November 1790

Ouders | gerret Neeffe | getuygen | David kerr
Eva Van houten | | en Egge Van houten
Naem Piter gebooren De 3 November gedoopt De 5 December 1790

ouders | Jan Doorremus | getuygen | De
Neuce Ryerson | | Vader en Moeder
Naem anaetye gebooren De 24 November gedoopt De 19 December 1790

Ouders | Tuenes Berdan | getuygen | Elisabeth Van Blercom en
Aeltye Van Blercom | | De Vader
Naem Jannetye gebooren De 16 November gedoopt De 19 December 1790

Ouders | Isack alyie | getuygen | De
Antye Ryerson | | Vader en Moeder
Naem David gebooren De 12 December 1790 gedoopt De 16 Janury 1791

Ouders | Johannes Van houten | getuygen | Cornelus Low
Sara Low | | trientye Claessen
Naem trientye gebooren De 11 December 1790 gedoopt De 16 January 1791

ouders | Piter Van houten | getuygen | De
Leya Van Rypen | | Vader en Moeder
Naem Leya gebooren De 28 December 1790 gedoopt De 30 January 1791

Ouders | Jan Van Blercom | getuygen | Vrowetye V Blercom
Antye Jacobosse | | en De Vader
Naem Annaetye gebooren De 6 January gedoopt De 13 february 1791

Ouders | Abraham Post | getuygen | Albert Zabrisko
Maria Zabrisko | | Jannetye Zabrisko
Naem Henderikes gebooren De 25 January gedoopt De 27 february 1791

Ouders | Simeon Van winkle | getuygen | De
Antye Merseles | | Vader en Moeder
Naem yanikke gebooren gedoopt De 27 March 1791

ouders | Abraham Van Rypen | getuygen | De Vader en
Altye Post | | Catrina Van blercom
Naem feytye gebooren De 11 January gedoopt De 27 March 1791

8

Ouders | Arant Schuyler / Ester Dey | getuygen | Ester De / Moeder Van De kinderen

De Naem Van De Eene was theunis Dey gebooren De 18 October 1785 De Andere was gebooren De 29 August 1788 Zyn naem was Piter gedoopt By Het huys Van Piter Dey March 27th 1791*

Ouders | Piter Dey / Lena Boerd | getuygen | De Vader en Jannetye / Post

Naem Ester gebooren De 30 November 1790 gedoopt De 27 March 1791

ouders | Jan Jacobosse / Eva Kipp | getuygen | Abram Jacobosse / en Elisabeth Jacobosse

Naem Abram gebooren De 14 March gedoopt De 10 April 1791

Ouders | Cornelus Westervelt / Maria Roblin | getuygen | De Vader en / Antye Westervelt

Naem trienye gebooren De 28 March gedoopt De 10 April 1791

ouders | Dirck Van giesen / Jannetye Van houten | getuygen | De / Vader en Moeder

Naem feytye gebooren De 29 March gedoopt De 24 April 1791

Ouders | David Dey / Sara Neeffe | getuygen | Johannes Neeffe / helena Dey

Naem helena gebooren De 31 March gedoopt De 15 May 1791

Ouders | Nicase Van blercom / Catrina Post | getuygen | gerrit Van Rypen / feytye westervelt

Naem John gebooren De 12 April gedoopt De 15 May 1791

ouders | Cornelus Post / Sara Dey | getuygen | De Vader en / Moeder

Naem Dirck Dey gebooren De 6 May gedoopt De 26 June 1791

ouders | abraham godwen / altye Van houten | getuygen | Jan Van orden / Jannetye V: houten

Namen Jannetye en Marretye gedoopt De 4 January 1788 twelingen

ouders | Johannes f Post / Antye Ratau | getuygen | Poules Ratau en / Jannetye Bord

Naem Poules gebooren De 14 July gedoopt De 7 Agustus 1791

ouders | Abraham godwin / Zyn wife | getuygen | De Vader en Moeder

Namen Van De kinderen Zyn Susanna Caleb Munson en Abraham Caleb Monson gebooren De 10th December 1788 Abraham is gebooren is gebooren De 14 July 1791 gedoopt De Drie kinderen Agustus De 21 1791†

Ouders | David hennion / Vrouwitye heunion | getuygen | De / Vader en Moeder

Naem Annetye gebooren De 23 July gedoopt De 21 Agustus 1791

---

*The name of the one was Theunis (Tunis) Dey, born October 18, 1785; the other was born August 29, 1788. His name was Peter. [Both were] baptized at the house of Peter Dey, March 27, 1791.

†Names of the children are Susanna, Caleb Munson and Abraham. Caleb Munson was born December 10, 1788. Abraham was born July 14, 1791. Baptized the three children August 21, 1791. [The date of Susanna's birth is not given. She died October 21, 1813. Abraham Godwin was a fifer in a New York Regiment during the Revolution, and subsequently was a General of Militia in New Jersey. His wife was Mary Munson. His son, Abraham, named above, also became a General of Militia, and was known as the "young General," to distinguish him from his father, the "old General." The deaths of the "old General" and his wife, and their daughter Susan, are mentioned on page 47, ante.]

ouders | Roelif C Van houten | getuygen | De vader
      | Aeltye Dooremus | | en Moeder
     Naem Ragel gebooren De 5 Agustus gedoopt De 18 September 1791

Ouders | Mathens Crauck | getuygen | Cornelus Van houten
      | geertruy Van houten | | en Metye V: houten
     Naem feytye gebooren De 1 September gedoopt De 2 october 1791

Ouders | Cornelus Van houten | getuygen | De
      | Maria Veeder | | Vader en Moeder
     Naem Antye gebooren De 18 Agustus gedoopt De 2 october 1791

ouders | Samuel Borhans | getuygen | De
      | Marregriet yeraleman | | Vader en Moeder
     Naem Jacobos gebooren De 20 October gedoopt 4 December 1791

Ouders | thunes hennion | getuygen | Leya kipp
      | Catrina kipp |
     Naem Leya geboren De 24 october gedoopt De 4 December 1791

Ouders | Daniel Ratan | getuygen | Johannis Ratan
      | Jannetye Brouwer | | en Zyn huysvrou
     Naem Johannes geboren De 25 May gedoopt De 10 June 1792

ouders | Benyamen Delemeter | getuygen | De
      | Claertye van houten | | Vader en Moeder
     Naem Sara geboren De 5 May gedoopt De 10 June 1792

Ouders | Abraham Post | getuygen | Abraham willis
      | Elisabeth hemmelton | | Catrina Post
     Naem Elksander McDukle* geboren De 8 June gedoopt De 5 Agustus
     1792

ouders | Ari Myer | getuygen | Jacob Storm
      | Susanna Storm | | Jannetye gerritse
     Naem grietye geboren De 30 July gedoopt de 9 September 1792

Ouders | Helmigh Van gieson | getuygen | Seel Van gieson
      | Sara van oeststrand | | antye Van gieson
     Naem Metye geboren De 20 Agustus gedoopt De 9 September 1792

ouders | Jacob Dooremus | getuygen | De
      | Myntye Van houten | | Vader en Moeder
     Naem Ragel geboren De 24 July gedoopt De 9 September 1792

Ouders | fince Chauler | getuygen | De
      | Sara MacCleen | | Vader en Moeder
     Naem Jonas geboren De 9 June gedoopt De 9 September 1792

Een kent gedoopt van Jan Moor genaemt Jan September 9th 1792

ouders | Albert Berdan | getuygen | De
      | Susanna | | Vader en Moeder
     Naem Susanna geboren De 25 September 1787 gedoopt De 22 Sep-
     tember 1792

Ouders | Albert Berdan | getuygen | De
      | Susanna | | Vader en Moeder
     Naem Albert geboren De 12 March 1789 gedoopt De 22 September
     1792

Ouders | Albert Berdan | getuygen | De
      | Susanna | | Vader en Moeder
     Naem Daniel geboren De 8 November 1790 gedoopt De 22 Septem-
     ber 1792

*Alexander McDougal.

Ouders | Abraham Vaudaun | getuygen | De
| Catriner Meath | | Veder en Moeder
Naem Salley geboren De 15 September gedoopt De 30 September 1792

ouders | Philip Dey | getuygen | De
| Jannetye Post | | Vader en Moeder
Naem Samuel bay gebooren De 28 August gedoopt De 30 September
1792

ouders | Andries Suyer | getuygen | Adam van orden
| Ragel ackerman | | Marregriet Suyer
Naem Doortte gebooren De 7 october gedoopt De 11 November 1792

Ouders | Jan Erven | getnygen | Hendriek Staag
| Elisebeth Staag | | Sara Post
Naem Sara gebooren De 7 September gedoopt D 11 November 1792

Ouders | Peter Jacobosse | getuygen | De Vader en Moeder
| Sara goold | |
Naem Jannicke gebooren De 1 May gedoopt De 11 November 1792

Ouders | John Cool | getuygen | De
| feytye Jacobosse | | Vader en Moeder
Naem Hendrick gebooren De 18 October gedoopt De 11 November
1792

Ouders | John Staag | getuygen | De
| Cornelia Van blercom | | Vader en Moeder
Naem David gebooren De 14 october gedoopt De 11 November 1792

Ouders | David Dey | getuygen | De
| Sara Neiffe | | Vader en Moeder
Naem tuenes gebooren De 12 October gedoopt De 2 December 1792

Ouders | tomes Suyder | getuygen | De
| Maria raten | | Vader en Moeder
Naem Jurre gebooren De 4 November gedoopt De 2 December 1792

ouders | John Simmons | getuygen | De Vader
| Mette Zyn vrou | | en Zyn Suster Maria
Naem abigel gebooren De 24 october gedoopt De 2 December 1792

Ouders | Joris Doorrinns | getuygen | De
| Antye Ratau | | Vader en Moeder
Naem Jennicke gebooren De 27 october gedoopt De 2 December 1792

ouders | Ellicksander Mc Coel | getuygen | De Vader en Moeder
| Ragel van blercom | |
Naem ertha* gebooren De 17 November gedoopt De 23 December 1792

ouders | Jan Spier | getuygen | Peter lock
| altye Ryker | | goertry Jacobosse
Naem Hester gebooren De 28 october gedoopt De 23 December 1792

ouders | John Ryerson | getuygen | De Vader
| Antye van aellen | | en Moeder
Naem Jannetye gebooren De 21 November gedoopt Do 30 December
1792

Ouders | Piter Duryeas | getuygen | Hendrick Demot
| Leya Mandeviel | | Elisabeth Mandeviel
Naem Elisabeth gebooren De 22 October gedoopt De 30 December
1792

—————

*Archie.

ouders | Cornelus Decker / en Zyn vrou | getuygen | Daniel Ratan / en Zyn vrou
Naem Daniel gebooren De 26 October gedoopt De 30 December 1792

ouders | Johannes kerstede / Lena Ryker | getuygen | Johannes Ryker / Leya Ryker
Naem Johannes gebooren De 9 December 1792 gedoopt De 13 January 1793

ouders | Hendrick Cook / annaetye Ryerson | getuygen | De / Vader en Moeder
Naem Sara gebooren De 16 October 1792 gedoopt De 13 January 1793

ouders | Jacob Demarest / geesye hopper | getuygen | Jacobos Demarest / en De vader en Moeder
Naem Jacobos gebooren De 4 January 1793 gedoopt De 3 february 1793

ouders | gerret van Derhoof / Soeke Zyn vrou | getuygen | De / Vader en Moeder
Naem Sara gebooren De 20 December 1792 gedoopt De 3 february 1793

ouders | Andris bomen / yannetye van houten | getuygen | De Vader / en Moeder
Naem Jacob gebooren De 3 January gedoopt De 3 february 1793

Ouders | David hennion / Antye kepp | getuygen | thunis hennion / Catrina kepp
Naem Vrouwetye gebooren De 3 January 1793 gedoopt De 3 february 1793

ouders | Isack van Saen / Catlyntye Merselus | getuygen | Samuel van Saen / Leya Zabriske
Naem Samuel gebooren De 6 January gedoopt De 3 february 1793

ouders | Jacobos van houten / Elisabeth Berri | getuygen | De / Vader en moeder
Naem Piter gebooren De 30 June 1792 gedoopt De 3 february 1793

Ouders | John hutten / Rachal Reynils | getuygen | Jacob Coopper / Elisabeth Sinirets
Naem Rachal gebooren De 2 July 1792 gedoopt De 3 february 1793

Ouders | Cornelus van Rypen / Vrouitye gerrotse | getuygen | De Vader en Moeder
Naem gerrebrant gebooren De 8 January gedoopt De 3 March.1793

ouders | adreyaen van houten / Marritye Cadmus | getuygen | Marten van blercom / Antye Zyn vrou
Naem Piter gebooren De 31 January gedoopt De 3 March 1793

Ouders | Dirck van houten / Ragel Post | getuygen | De / vader en Moeder
Naem Piter gebooren De 28 January gedoopt De 3 March 1793

Ouders | Hendrick Cook / yannetye Pier | getuygen | De Vader / en Moeder
Naem Sara gebooren De 12 february gedoopt De 17 Mert 1793

ouders | Albert Berdan / Susanna Secord | getuygen | De vader / en Moeder
Naem Jacob gebooren De 30 January gedoopt De 17 Mert 1793

Ouders | Jaen Cool / Elisabeth Lutkins | getuygen | Baarnt Cool / ketrienna van De waters Zyn Vrou
Naem Barnt gebooren De 24 february gedoopt De 17 Mert 1793

onders | gerrit Neeffe / Catlyntye post | getuygen | De vader · / en Moeder
Naem Johannes gebooren De 6 february gedoopt De 1 April 1793

onders | Johannes hinnion / Phebe Boalden | getuygen | De Vader / en Moeder
Naem Abraham gebooren De 29 May 1792 gedoopt De 1 April 1793

onders | Cornelus van houten / feytye van houten | getuygen | De / vader en Moeder
Naem Marretye gebooren De 9 february gedoopt De 1 April 1793

Ouders | Piter Zealif / Zyn vrou Ryker | getuygen | De / vader en Moeder
Naem   geboouen De   gedoopt De 1 April 1793

Ouders | Albert Zabrisko / Aeltye van orden | getuygen | De vader / en Elisabeth goetsyes
Naem   geboouen De 13 february gedoopt De 1 April 1793

Ouders | Jacobos Jacobosse / Catrina Demerest | getuygen | De / vader en Moeder
Naem annetye geboouen De 25 october 1791 gedoopt De 1 April 1793

Ouders | Hendrick Jacobosse / Sara Sisko | getuygen | De Moeder
Naem gerrit geboouen De 16 Agustus 1791 gedoopt De 1 April 1793

ouders | Matheus Cranck / geertruy van houten | getuygen | De Vader en Moeder
Naem Maria geboouen De 14 March gedoopt De 21 April 1793

ouders | Martin Bruyn / Naetye Post | getuygen | De vader en Moeder
Naem Joannes geboouen De 4 November 1792 gedoopt De 21 April 1793

onders | Jan van blercom / Antye Jacobosse | getuygen | Derck Durie / Marritye Jacobosse
Naem Jacobos geboouen De 28 Mart gedoopt De 9 May 1793

onders | John More / Catrienua M Clien | getuygen | De / Vader en Moeder
Naem Cornelus geboouen De 8 Mert gedoopt De 9 May 1793

Ouders | Johannes Ryerson / Neuce Erchable* | getuygen | De / vader en Moeder
Naem Lena geboouen De   gedoopt De 9 May 1793

onders | Johannes van winkel / Elisabeth Ryerson | getuygen | De / vader en Moeder
Naem Maria DeBoos geboouen De 5 April gedoopt De 9 May 1793

ouders | Daniel van horn / Annaetye Erl | getuygen | De / vader en Moeder
Naem Annaetye geboouen De 30 Martch gedoopt De 9 June 1793

Ouders | Braut Jacobosse / titye van Duyn | getuygen | De / vader en Moeder
. Naem Jacobos geboouen De 12 May gedoopt De 30 June 1793

Query: Archibald?

ouders | Jan hencok / Jannetye van blercom | getuygen | De vader en Moeder
Naem tomas gebooren De 7 June gedoopt De 30 June 1793

Ouders | Hendrick Monerse / Catrina Alyi | getuygen | De vader en Moeder
Naem Catrina gebooren De 19 January gedoopt De 30 June 1793

Ouders | Robbert M Cael / Elisabeth Chappel | getuygen | De vader en Moeder
Naem Ercha* gebooren De 21 March gedoopt De 30 June 1793

Ouders | Abraham Jacobosse / Leya Mandeveel | getuygen | De vader en Moeder
Naem Jacobos geboren De 12 May gedoopt De 30 June 1793

ouders | Abraham Willis / Catrina Post | getuygen | De vader en Moeder
Naem Maria gebooren De 17 May gedoopt De 30 June 1793

Ouders | Roelif Doorremus / Annaetye Dooremus | getuygen | De Vader en Moeder
Naem Catrina gebooren De 30 May gedoopt de 30 June 1793

Ouders | Jan Dooremus / Antye Ryerson | getuygen | De Vader en Moeder
Naem Hendrick gebooren De 3 May gedoopt De 30 June 1793

Ouders | gilyaem Ryerson / Marigrietye Mannen | getuygen | De vader en Moeder
Naem Ryer gebooren De 30 June gedoopt de 11 Augustus 1793

ouders | Abraham Ryerson / Sara Mandeviel | getuygen | De vader en Moeder
Naem Elisabeth gebooren De 1 July gedoopt De 11 Augustus 1793

ouder | Catrina Stegg | getuygen | Johannes Ryker / Jannetye Stegg
Naem Jacobos gebooren De 2 November 1792 gedoopt De 11 Augustus 1793

†Ouders | Helmaugh Post / Metye Van Riper | getuygen | De vader en Moeder
Naem thomas gebooren De 14 Agustes gedoopt De 1 september 1793

ouders | Hendrick Hennion / Maria Romine | getuygen | De Vader en Moeder
Naem Cornalious gebooren De 14 Agustes gedoopt De 1 September 1793

onders | Cornelious Van Houten / maria Vater | getuygen | De vader en Moeder
Naem maria Gebooren De 14 Agustes gedoopt De 1 September 1793

ouders | Peter Van Howten / Leyen Van Ripen | getuygen | De Vader en Moeder
Naem Peter geboren De 30 yuli Gedoopt De 1 September 1793

ouders | hous Post / maretye Neafe | getuygen | De Vader en moder
Naem Aultye geborer De 29 yuli gedoopt De 1 September 1793

---

*Archie.

†Beginning here a new hand began keeping the record, and one evidently not so well educated as his predecessor, as appears by various eccentricities in chirography and orthography.

Ouders | Davit Griffins / Sara forse | getuygen | De Vader / en moder
Naem Janneyo   Geboren De 10 Augustes   Gedoopt de 1 September 1793

ouders | John Berdon / leau sine huis vrouw | getuygen | De vader / en moder
Naem Henderick   Geboren De 22 Yuly   Gedoopt De 1 September 1793

Ouders | Davit Hennion / vrouwetja Hennion | getuygen | De Vader en / moder
Naem marigreje   Geboren De 3 Augustes   Gedoopt De 1 September 1793

Ouders | Yon Speir / Abbe Van Busse | De Getnigen | Abraham Van Ripen en sin huis / vrow Dose Westervelt
Naem Tennis   Geboren De 24 September   Gedoopt De 13 October 1793

Ouders | Garret Neafe / Even Van Houten | De Getuigen | De Vader / en moder
Naem Annante   Geboren De 22 September   Gedoopt De 13 October 1793

Ouders | Robert Van Houten / Lenaw Van giason | getuigen | De / Vader en moder
Naem Rolef   Geboren De 16 September   Gedoopt De 13 October 1793

Ouders | Yon yecobesa / Even Kip | De Getnigen | Necense Kip / Leau maudferviel
Naem Leau   Geboren De 12 September   Gedoopt De 13 October 1793

Ouders | Abraham ackerman / Elisebath Kronk | getuigen | De Vader en / Moder
Naem Yanate   Geboren De 7 September   Gedoopt De 13 October 1793

Ouders | Yon leshere / Pege hill | getuigen | De Vader en / Moder
Naem Cornelius   Geboren De 8 Mey   Gedoopt De 13 October 1793

Ouders | Johannes van Rypen / Leya kipp | getuygen | De / vader en Moeder
Naem Gerrit   gebooren De 6 october   gedoopt De 3 November 1793

Ouders | Tomes Hemmon / Elisebeth Romjne | getnigen | De / Vader en Moder
Naem Abraham   gebooren De 22 Yune   gedoopt De 3 November 1793

Ouders | William Brower / Marija sine huys Vrow | getnjgen | De / Vader en Moder
Naem kestejnye   gebooren De 23 September   Gedopt de 3 November 1793

Ouders | Johannes Toars / Marigrit Kipp | Getnjgen | Isaac Kipp / heinke* Van Geison
Naem Isaac   gebooren De 8 October   Gedopt De 3 November 1793

Ouders | Adreyaen Post / Sara Spier | getuygen | De / vader en Moeder
Naem Elias   gebooren De 1 October 1791   gedoopt De 17 November 1793

Ouders | Roelif Romyn / Bregge van Devoort | getuygen | De vader / en Moeder
Naem Maria   gebooren De 6 October   gedoopt De 17 November 1793

*Query: Hank, Hen., Henry?

Ouders | Piter van houten | getuygen | Roelif van houten
Marregriet Botteler | | Aeltye Dooremus
Naem James gebooren De 27 Agustus gedoopt De 17 November 1793

ouders | Jan Blercom | getuygen | De
Maria Jacobosse | | vader en Moeder
Naem Elias gebooren De 15 November gedoopt De 8 December 1793

ouders | frans Ryerson | getuygen | De
Jannetye Lambert | | vader en Moeder
Naem Jannetye gebooren De 6 November gedoopt De 8 December
1793

Ouders | William Mills | getuygen | De vader en het wyf
Antye Ennes | | van george annes
Naem Neeltye gebooren De 19 November 1792 gedoopt De 8 December
1793

ouders | Dyldrick van Rypen | getuygen | De
annecke Dooremus | | Vader en Moeder
Naem gerrit gebooren De 1 September gedoopt De 25 December 1793

onders | Johannes gerritse | getuygen | De
Marregriet van Rypen | | Vader en Moeder
Naem Hendrick gebooren De 19 November gedoopt De 25 December
1793

Ouders | Hendrick Dooremus | getuygen | De
Marregriet hennion | | Vader en Moeder
Naem Hendrick gebooren De 17 December 1793 gedoopt De 19 January 1794

ouders | Jan Ryerson | getuygen | De
Leya Westervelt | | Vader en Moeder
Naem Jores gebooren De 17 December 1793 gedoopt De 19 January
1794

Ouders | Albert Alye | getuygen | Antye Ryerson
Dalle Snyder | | en de vader
Naem Albert gebooren De 24 December 1793 gedoopt De 19 January
1794

ouders | Roelif van houten | getuygen | De
Antye van giesen | | vader en Moeder
Naem Metye gebooren De 7 January gedoopt De 9 February 1794

Ouders | Jan Pules | getuygen | De
Sally hand | | vader en Moeder
Naem Elisabeth gebooren De 1 December gedoopt De 9 february
1794

Ouders | gerrit gerritse | getuygen | gerrit gerritse
Lena Scoonmaker | | fytye westervelt
Naem gerrit gebooren De 5 february gedoopt De 2 Mert 1794

Ouders | Roelif van houten | getuygen | Hessel Piterse
Autye Berdan | | fytye van houten
twelingen | | Adreyaen Post
Namen feytye & Maria | | Maria Berdan
gebooren De 26 January gedoopt De 2 Mert 1794

ouders | Nicase van blercom | getuygen | Helmigh van houten
Catrina Post | | Lena van Blercom
Naem Antye gebooren De 24 January gedoopt De 2 Mert 1794

9

onders | Dirck van houten | getnygen | Jan Neeffe
       | Ragel Post | | Catrina Post
    Naem John gebooren De 1 february gedoopt De 2 Mert 1794

Onders | Abram freland | getuygen |
       | Annaetye Moor | |
    Naem Polle gebooren De 10 Agustus 1793 gedoopt De 2 Mert 1794

Onders | John van Rypen | getnygen | Jan Romyn
       | Sara Romyn | | Lena Stagg
    Naem Nickolas gebooren De 14 March gedoopt De 20 february 1794

Onders | hons Westervelt | De getuijgen | Yacob acerman
       | Leow Pervo | | en sine vrow
    Naem Jacob Geboren De 17 February Gedoopt De 6 Apprill 1794

Ouders | Horremann Van order | De getnijgen | Jon Westervelt
       | Fite Westervelt | | Ante Van Riper
    Naem Yamaee Geboren 18 Mart Gedoopt De 6 Apprjl 1794

Onders | Isaae Kronk | De Getnygen | De
       | Janate Van Houten | | Vader en Moder
    Naem Abraham Geboren De 6 Mart Gedoopt De 6 Apprjl 1794

Onders | Corneljons Van Rjper | De Getnygen | De
       | Elysebeth Van Rjper | | Vader en Moder
    Naem Cotreman Geboren De 24 Mart Gedoopt De 21 Apprjl 1794

Onders | Abraham Van Blercom | De Getnygen | hendrie Van Blercom
       | Vromaty Van Blercom | | Marja Van Blercom
    Naem Annanji Geboren De 29 Mart Gedoopt De 21 April 1794

*Ouders | Albert Zabrisko | getny,gen | De
        | Aeltye van orden | | Vader en Moeder
    Naem Hendrick gebooren De 19 April gedoopt De 9 June 1794

Onders | Edo Merselis | getuygen | Simion van winkel
       | Lena van houten | | Antye Merselis
    Naem Jennicke gebooren De 15 April gedoopt De 9 June 1794

onders | David Dey | getuygen | De
       | Sara Neeffe | | Vader en Moeder
    Naem annaetye gebooren De 23 April gedoopt De 29 June 1794

Onders | Jan herres | getuygen | De
       | Marregriet van horn | | Vader en Moeder
    Naem Catrina gebooren De 15 May gedoopt De 29 June 1794

onders | hendrick herris | getuygen | Johannes Berdan
       | Neesye van horn | | Maria De gra
    Naem Maria gebooren De May gedoopt De 29 June 1794

ouders | Abraham Brower | getuygen | De
       | feytye Jacobosse | | Vader en Moeder
    Naem Johannes gebooren De 25 february gedoopt De 29 June 1794
    By Zyn huys

onders | Jan Stagg | getuygen | Jan Romyn
       | Elisabeth Romyn | | grietye fecok
    Naem grietye gebooren De 13 May gedoopt De 20 July 1794

Ouders | Coenraat Row | getuygen | Ponlis van Devoort
       | Catrina Ryker | | Elisabeth Rijker
    Naem Willem geboren De 22 May gedoopt De 20 July 1794

---

*Beginning here, the record is in the same handwriting as that for many years
next-preceding September, 1793.

Ouders | Jores Dooremus | getuygen | De
| Antye Ratan | | vader en Moeder
  Naem Catrina gebooren De 24 July gedoopt De 10 Agustus 1794

Ouders | David Romyn | getuygen | Piter Storr
| Jannetye van Debeek | | Sara van Winkel
  Naem John gebooren De 1 June gedoopt De 10 Agustus 1794

Ouders | Jacob Dooremus | getuygen | De
| Meyntye van houten | | Vader en Moeder
  Naem Cornelus gebooren De 20 July gedoopt De 31 Agustus 1794

Ouders | Megiel Boss | getuygen | Jacob Soots
| Antye Smit | | Antye Boss
  Naem Leya gebooren De 26 July gedoopt De 31 Agustus 1794

Ouders | Abram van houten | getuygen | De
| Maria Botler | | Vader en Moeder
  Naem grietye gebooren De 27 Agustus gedoopt De 21 September 1794

Ouders | tuenes Berdan | getuygen | De
| Aeltye van Blercom | | vader en Moeder
  Naem Elisabeth gebooren De 25 Agustus gedoopt De 21 September
  1794

Ouders | ari Post | getuygen | De
| Maria Stagg | | Vader en Moeder
  Naem Helmigh gebooren De 8 Agustus gedoopt De 21 September 1794

Ouders | John Hutten | getuygen | De
| Ragel Rennels* | | Vader en Moeder
  Naem Henne gebooren De 21 Agustus gedoopt De 21 September 1794

ouders | Hendrick kipp | getuygen | De vader en Moeder
| Catrina Dooremus |
  Naem Egge gebooren De 2 September gedoopt De 21 September 1794

Ouders | Abraham gerritse | getuygen | De
| Jannetye hennion | | vader en Moeder
  Naem Jacob gebooren De 6 September gedoopt De 9 October 1794

Ouders | george mousen | getuygen | De Moeder
| annaetye van houten |
  Naem Isack gebooren De 13 September 1789 gedoopt De 9 October
  17[94]†

ouders | tomas Dooremus | getuygen | De
| Elisabeth van houten | | Vader en Moeder
  Naem Daniel gebooren De 30 Agustus gedoopt De 12 october 1794

ouders | David kerr | getuygen | De
| Antye Westervelt | | vader en Moeder.
  Naem Elisabeth gebooren De 12 September gedoopt De 12 october
  1794

ouders | Bryant Shass‡ | getuygen | De
| Anny Duvall | | vader en Moeder
  Naem Joseph Warren gebooren De 23 June gedoopt De 12 october
  1794

*Rachel Reynolds.

†Some of the leaves are so worn away on the margins that figures and words are gone; where they have been conjecturally supplied they are inclosed in brackets.

‡Bryant Sheys, a tavern-keeper and afterwards for many years a school-teacher in and about Paterson.

ouders | Isack van Saen
Catelyntye Merselis | getuygen | Jan Merselis
Jannetye van Rypen
Naem Jennecke gebooren De 23 September gedoopt De 12 october 1794

ouders | Albert van Saen
Jannetye van houten | getuygen | Samuel van Saen
Leya Zabrisco
Naem Maria gebooren De 19 September gedoopt De 12 october 1794

ouders | David Carns
Elisebeth van voorhesen | getuygen | De
vader en Moeder
Naem Corneliya gebooren De 13 September gedoopt De 2 November 1794

Ouders | David Ackerman
Matte Ernist | getuygen | Jan Erl
Ragel ackerman
Naem Jacomyn gebooren De 20 october gedoopt De 2 November 179[4]

ouders | gerrit Brower
Lena Spier | getuygen | De vader en Moeder
Naem Johannes gebooren De 6 September gedoopt De 2 November 1794

ouders | Jacob van Rypen
Abigel Loris | getuygen | De
vader en Moeder
Naem Rachel gebooren De 6 September gedoopt De 2 November 1794

ouders | Isack Pier
Maria post | getuygen | Jacobos post
Sara Dey
Naem francoos gebooren De 25 September gedoopt De 2 November 179[4]

Onders | Poulis Ratan
Metye Spier | getuygen | Jan toers
Lybe Ratan
Naem Poulis gebooren De 23 Agustus gedoopt De 2 November 1794

Ouders | Direk Dey
Annaetye pierson | getuygen | De
Vader en Moeder
Naem William Mac adams gebooren De   gedoopt De 2 November 1794

Ouders | gerrit gerritse
grietye van Rypen | getuygen | gerrebrant Bruijn
Catrina van Rypen
Naem Catrina gebooren De 25 October gedoopt De 14 December 1794

Ouders | Helmigh van giesen
Sara ostronder | getuygen | Johannes van giesen en
Metye van houten
Naem Johannes gebooren De 25 December 1794 gedoopt De 18 January 1795

onders | John Berdan
Lena Bruyn | getuygen | De
vader en Moeder
Naem Jacob gebooren De 2 January gedoopt De 8 february 1795

onders | Abram Spier
Sara vanDerhoof | getuygen | De
Vader en Moeder
Naem Sara gebooren De 17 November 1794 gedoopt De 8 february 1795

Ouders | Albert Berdan
Susanna Secord | getuygen | De
vader en Moeder
Naem Samuel gebooren De 28 December 1794 gedoopt De 22 february 1795

*Ouders | semion Van Blarcom | Getuigen | De Vader
bragje Van Blarcom | | en Moder
Naem John Geboren De 14 february gedoopt De 15 Mart 1795

Ouders | Peter Acemant | Getuigen | De
Nanje Vrelant | | Vader En Moder
Naam Peter Geboren D 24 february ged opt De 15 Mart 1795

Ouders | Tennis Speer | Getuigen | Henderick mandervicl
Rachel mandervicl | | lenew mandervicl
Naem lenew Geboren De 28 february gedoopt De [5 April 1795]

Ouders | Jon aerl | Getuijgen | Davit Acerman
Rachel Acerman | | Matye arnist
Naem Matye Geboren De 12 Mart Gedopt De 5 Appril 1795

ouders | Cornelious Kipp | getuijgen | Aurint sgniler‖
tjue Demoreyt | | Rachel Demorey
Twelinge | | en Corneljus Kipp tene Demorey
Naem Rachel en marjgritye Geboren De 15 Mart Gedopt De 5 Appril
1795

Ouders | Thunis Spear | getuijgen | De vader en Moeder
goesye Everse | |
Naem Hendrick geboren De 24 Mert gedoopt de 19 April 1795

Ouders | Gerrit Neafi | getuygen | De vader en Moder
Catljne Post | |
Naem francose Geboren De 7 Mart Gedopt De 19 Aprill 1795

Ouders | Cornelyous Merselus | getuygen | De Vader en Moder
Marya Post | |
Naem Edo Geboren De 18 Mart Gedopt De 19 Apyll 1795

Ouder | Jacob Dooremus | Getuijgen | De
Neltyi Peir | | Vader en Moder
Naem Johonis Geboren De 26 february Gedopt De 19 April 1795

ouders | Chrisstopher Brower | getuygen | De
Lena van houten | | vader en Moeder
Naem Maria geboren De 16 April gedoopt De 7 May 1795

ouders | Benyaman Delemater | getuygen | De
Claertye van houten | | vader en Moeder
Naem Elisabeth geboren De 23 Mart gedoopt De 24 May 1795

Ouders | David Deves | getuygen | De
Leya Merceker | | vader en Moeder
Naem tomas gebooren De 20 April gedoopt De 7 June 1795

ou lers | Jan Dooremus | getuygen | Bill Dierman
geertye Ryerson | | griety Dooremus
Naem grietye gebooren De 25 April gedoopt De 7 June 1795

ouders | David Brower | getuygen | David Brower
Sara Remmer | | Arreyaenye Stymets
Naem David gebooren De 20 May gedoopt De 28 June 1795

*Beginning here, the next nine entries are in the same handwriting as those of October 13—November 3, inclusive, 1793.

†Ackerman,

‡Demarest.

‖Arent Schuyler.

ouders | William Decker / Aeltye Myor | getuygen | De / vader en Moeder
Naem Marten gebooren De 13 May gedoopt De 28 June 1795

ouders | Andris hopper / Aeltye ackerman | getuygen | Jan hopper / Maria westervelt
Naem Aeltye gebooren De 1 June gedoopt De 28 June 1795

ouders | Johannes post / Antye Ratan | getuygen | De / vader en Moeder
Naem Bregge gebooren De 4 April gedoopt De 28 June 1795

ouders | Ari Boss / Sytye Mowerse | getuygen | De vader en Moeder
Naem Elisabeth gebooren De 7 June gedoopt De 28 June 1795

Ouders | Abraham witten / Catrina Blavelt | getuygen | Joseph witten • / Catlyntye Miller
Naem Joseph gebooren De 14 June gedoopt De 19 July 1795

ouders | Piter Merselious / Janete Van Winele | Getuygen | De / Vader En Moder
Naem Johones Geboren De 23 Agustus gedoopt De 20 September 1795

ouders | Cornelus T Doorremus / Jannetye van orden | getuygen | De vader en Moeder
Naem Selle gebooren De 25 Agustus gedoopt De 20 September 1795

Ouders | Jan Jacobosse / Eva kipp | getuygen | De vader en / Leya kipp
Naem Eva gebooren De 11 July gedoopt De 1 November 1795

ouders | Johannes Bensen / Maria westervelt | getuygen | De / vader en Moeder
Naem Sofya gebooren De 20 October gedoopt De 1 November 1795

ouders | Josey Brower / en Zyn wife | getuygen | De / vader en Moeder
Naem Daniel gebooren De 23 September gedoopt De 1 November 1795

ouders | David Cerr / Antye westervelt | getuygen | De vader / en Moeder
Naem Johannes gebooren De 23 Agustus gedoopt De 1 November 1795

ouders | Abraham Vrelant / Ane More | getuygen | gerrit Vrelant / Ragel Moor
Naem gerrit gebooren De 24 Agustus gedoopt De 1 November 1795

ouders | Jan Van Houten / Maria Brower | getuygen | David Brower / Areyaenye Stymets
Naem Areyaentye gebooren De 12 October gedoopt De 1 November 1795

ouders | Cornelus Van Rypen / Vrouwetye gerritse | getuygen | De Vader / en Moeder
Naem gerrit gebooren De 15 September gedoopt De 1 November 1795

ouders | William wite / Catrina Ryker | getuygen | De Vader / en Moeder
Naem Marregriet gebooren De 29 July gedoopt De 1 November 1795

Ouders | Jacob Steek / Maria Andrews | getuygen | De Vader en / Sara Ratan
Naem Jacob gebooren De 24 Agustus gedoopt De 22 November 1795

ouders | David godwin | getuygen | Adolf Waldron
Catrina Waldron | | Elisabeth Waldron
Naem Abraham Resolve gebooren De 8 Novemb   gedoopt De 22
November 1795

ouders | Johannes Van winkel | getuygen | De Vader
Elisabeth Ryerson | | en Moeder
Naem Johannes Jores Ryerson gebooren De 1 November gedoopt De
6 December 1795

ouders | francoos Ryorson | getuygen | De Vader
Jannetye Lambert | | en Leya Lambert
Naem francoos gebooren De 15 November gedoopt De 6 December
1795

ouders | Albert Alye | getuygen | John Potter
Dalle Snyder | | Maria Smit
Naem Adam gebooren De 6 November gedoopt De 6 December 1795

ouders | Johannes van blercom | getuygen | De
Antye Jacobosse | | vader en Moeder
Naem gerritye gebooren De 16 November gedoopt De 25 December
1795

ouders | Harmanes Bross | getuygen | Harmanes Bross
Catrina Ellens | | en Jannetye Bross
Naem Luykes gebooren D 6 December gedoopt De 25 December 1795

ouders | Helmigh Van houten | getuygen | De
Lena van blercom | | Vader en Moeder
Naem Johannes gbooren De 9 December 1795 gedoopt De 1 January
1796

ouders | Cornelus westervelt | getuygen | De Vader en Moeder
Maria Roblin | |
Naem Abraham gebooren De 16 Decembr 1795 gedoopt De 1 January
1796

ouders | David Benson | getuygen | De Vader en Moeder
Elisabeth van houten | |
Naem Johannes gebooren De 27 December 1795 gedoopt De 17 January 1796

ouders | Jan hencock | getuygen | De
Jannetye van blercom | | Vader en Moeder
Naem William gebooren De 7 September 1795 gedoopt De 17 January
1796

ouders | David Dooremus | getuygen | De Vader
Elisabeth van houten | | en Moeder
Naem Elisabeth gebooren De 23 December 1795 gedoopt De 7 february 1796

ouders | Lodewyck Merceker | getuygen | De vader
Sara Spier | | en Aelly Spier
Naem John gebooren De 1 January gedoopt De 7 february 1796

ouders | Robert van houten | getuygen | De Vader en Moeder
Lena van gieson | |
Naem Metye gebooren De 21 January gedoopt De 28 february 1796

ouders | gerrebrant Bruin | getuygen | gerrebrant gerrisse
Catrina Van Derhoef | | Antye Bruin
Naem Antye gebooren De 27 January gedoopt De 28 february 1796

ouders | Daniel van hoorn | getuygen | De
         | Annaetye Erl | | Vader en Moeder
Naem Daniel gebooren De 29 January gedoopt De 28 february 1796

ouders | John tures | getuygen | De
         | Lyba Ratau | | vader en Moeder
Naem Poules geboooren De 30 January gedoopt De 28 february 1796

Ouders | Nicholas Cokoro | getuygen | De
         | Piterye van Blercom | | vader en Moeder
Naem Polly geboooren De 17 february gedoopt De 20 March 1796

ouders | thunis Hennion | getuygen | Johaunes hennion
         | Sofya witte | | Elisabeth Berry
Naem Elisabeth geboooren De 18 february gedoopt De 20 March 1796

ouders | John Sigler | getuygen | De Vader
         | Siche Mandeveel | | en Moeder
Naem Rachel geboooren De 7 January gedoopt De 20 March 1796

ouders | Cornelus gerrebrautse | getuygen | De Vader
         | Maria Ryker | | en Moeder
Naem Piter geboooren De 14 January gedoopt De 20 March 1796

ouders | Johaunes Van Rypen | getuygen | Vader en
         | Leya kipp | | De Moeder
Naem Nicknse geboooren De 9 february gedoopt De 3 April 1796

ouders | Johaunes Ryker | getuygen | De
         | Mertynye Dooremus | | Vader en Moeder
Naem   geboooren De 12 february gedoopt De 3 April 1796

ouders | Cornelus H Post | getuygen | Jurre Suyder
         | Jannetye van Houten | | Sara van houten
Naem Aeltye geboooren De 22 November 1795 gedoopt De 3 April
1796

Ouders | Jacobos Van houten | getuygen | De Vader
         | Maria Banta | | en Moeder
Naem Jacob geboooren De 7 Mert gedoopt De 3 April 1796

ouders | Jan Brower | getuygen | gerrit wyt
         | griety wyt | | grietye Brower
Naem Lena geboooren De 3 April gedoopt De 24 April 1796

ouders | Johannes Post | getnygen | De
         | Elisabeth Ackerman | | Vader en Moeder
Naem Louwerens geboooren De 25 December gedoopt De 24 April 1796

ouders | Jacobus Ackerman | getuygen | Louwerens Ackerman
         | Catlyntye Post | | Annaetye van houten
Naem Catlyntye geboooren De 15 february gedoopt De 24 April 1796

May 12th 1796 is gedoopt Elisabeth yeomen De Vrow van David Spier in
De kerk Van Totowa geboooren De 24 May 1778

ouders | David Spier | getuygen | De Vader
         | Elisabeth yeoman | | en Moeder
Naem feytye geboooren De 6 March gedoopt De 15 May 1796

ouders | Cristiyaen Scoort | getuygen | De
         | grietye Demarest | | Vader en Moeder
Naem William geboooren De 20 April gedoopt De 15 May 1796

ouders | John Ryker | getuygen | De
         | Jannetye Stagg | | Vader en Moeder
Naem Willem geboooren De 21 March gedoopt De 15 May 1796

Ouders | David Romyn / Jannetye van Debeck | getuygen | John Stagg / Elisabeth Romyn
Naem Sara geboren De 19 Mert gedoopt De 15 May 1796

Ouders | John Puellis / Sara hen | getuygen | De Vader en Moeder
Naem Eva geboren De 25 April gedoopt De 15 May 1796

ouders | John Sindel / grietye Coesstede | getuygen | John Coesstedo / Sara Jacobosse
Naem John geboren De 22 Mert gedoopt De 15 May 1796

ouders | Roelif Van houten / Antye Van gieson | getuygen | De Vader en Moeder
Naem Johannes geboren De 14 May gedoopt De 29 May 1796

onders | David Hennion / Vrouwitye Hennion | getuygen | David Brower / Arreyaenye Stymets en De vader en Moeder
Namen David en Vrouwitye geboren De 21 April gedoopt De 29 May twelinggen 1796

ouders | Cornelus Van houten / Maria Veder | getuygen | De Vader en Moeder
Naem Jacob geboren De 18 April gedoopt De 29 May 1796

*Ouders | Albert Zabrjske / Aultye Van order | getuygen | De Vader en Moeder
Naem yannjty geboren De 5 May gedopt De 19 June 1796

Ouders | Jon Ridgwey / Pegey Acermen | getuygen | De Vader en Moder
Naem Sara geboren De 31 Apprill gedopt De 19 June 1796

Ouders | Mathew Crack / geertruy van houten | getuygen | De vader en Moder
Naem Egge geboren De 14 May gedoopt De 31 July 1796

Ouders | Jacob Quacinbus / maria Pake | Getuygen | De vader en Moder
Naem Jon Geboren De 22 Agustis Gedopt De 11 september 1796

onders | Henderick Hennion / Maria Romine | Getuygen | De Vader En Moder
Naem Elesebeth Geboren De 8 July Gedopt De 11 September 1796

Ouders | Peter Demorey / Tyne Benson | Getnjgen | Jacobus Westervelt / Elesebeth Demorey
Naem Elesebeth Geboren De 4 September Gedopt De 2 October 1796

Ouders | Isaac Blawvelt / Sara Jonson | Getuygen | De Vader en Moder
Naem Joseph Geboren De 15 September Gedopt De 2 October 1796

Ouders | lias Yorks / Ragel Rycer | Getuygen | De Vader en Moder
Naem leeu Geboren De 2 Augustes Gedopt De 23 October 1796

Ouders | Isaac Cronk / Jannete Van Houten | Getuygen | De Vader En Moder
Naem marca Geboren 25 July Gedopt De 23 October 1796

*The remainder of the record, covering a period of twelve years, is in the handwriting of the person who kept it October 13–November 3, 1793, and during February and March, 1795. He had an orthographical system of his own for spelling names, and adhered to it with a pernicious consistency.

Ouders | Abraham Van Houten | Getuygen | Rolef Van Houten
feytye Van Houten | | En Elesebeth Dooremus
Naem Jacob Geboren De 26 September Gedopt De 23 October 1796

Ouders | brjent shays | Getuygen | haus Post
Annaye Duvall | | Jannate Post
Naem Tomas Geboren De 14 Augustes Gedopt De 13 November 1796

Ouders | deric H Van Houten | Getuygen | De Vader
Ragel Post | | En Moder
Naem Corneliaus Geboren De 4 October Gedopt De 13 November 1796

Ouders | Henderee Van Blarcom | Getuygen | De
Derece Acerman | | Vader En Moder
Naem Annatite Geboren De 22 October Gedopt De 13 November 1796

Ouders | Harremoness Van Order | Getuygen | Jon Reyerson
fyte Westervelt | | Leen Westervelt
Neam Leen Geboren De 8 October Gedopt De 13 November 1796

Ouders | Jores Doorremus | Getuygen | Lious tice
Even yong | | Marye yong
Naem Marya Geboren De 3 October Gedopt De 13 November 1796

Ouders | Peter Olye | Getuygen | De Vader En Moder
Elesebeth Mouerse | |
Naem Jacob Geboren De 3 Augustes Gedopt De 13 November 1796

Ouders | David P' Harring | Getuygen | De
Trynte Gerebrause | | Vader En Moder
Naem Jon Geboren De 24 September Gedopt De 4 December 1796

Ouders | Jon Courte | Getuygen | De
Cantrenen Hensompecer | | Vader En Moder
Naem Willem Geboren De 10 November Gedopt De 4 December 1796

Ouders | Jacob Van Derbake | Getuygen | Poulis Vander Bake
Anneuje Vus | | Pegje Vus
Neam Gerteren Geboren De 9 October Gedopt De 4 December 1796

Ouders | Edo Merselus | Getuygen | Cornelious Van Houten
Lenen Van Houten | | Matje Van Houten
Naem Cornelious Geboren De 7 November Gedopt De 25 December 1796

ouders | Henderic Kipp | Getuygen | Cornelious Kip
Catrenen Dooremus | | Tyne Demorey
Naem Cristenen Geboren De 27 October Gedopt de 25 December 1796

Ouders | Johones H Gerreson | Getuygen | De
Marregretye Van Rjpen | | Vader En Moder
Naem Henderic Geboren De 20 November Gedopt De 25 December 1796

Ouders | Gorrit Brower | Getuygen | De
Lenen Speir | | Vader En Moder
Naem Gesce Geboren De 26 October Gedopt De 25 December 1796

Ouders | Jerrey yerrejanse | Getuygen | Caurl Devoise
Elesebeth van Blercom | | Jacemjne Van horn
Naem Jacemine Geboren De 27 December Gedopt De 29 Janewarey 1797

Ouders | Rulef Van Houten / Antye Berdou | Getuygen | Jacobos Post / Janetye Van Geson
Naem Catreneu Geboren De 22 December Gedopt De 29 Janewarey 1797

Ouders | Jan Dooremus / Geertruy Ryersou | Getuygen | De Vader En Moder
Naem Geertruy Geboren De 26 December Gedopt De 29 Janewarey 1797

Ouders | Albert Van Sann / Janetye Van Houten | Getuygen | De Vader Eu Moder
Naem Elesebeth Geboren De 24 Jannawary Gedopt De 19 Fabruary 1797

Ouders | Helmugh Van Geason / salley Van Ostronder | Getuygen | De Vader En Moder
Naem Crisstufel Geboren De 16 Janewary Gedopt De 19 Fabruarey 1797

Ouders | Jacob Dooremus / Jacemine Van Houten | Getuygen | De Vader En Moder
Naem Jacob Geboren De 28 December Gedopt De 19 Februarey 1797

Ouders | Steveunus Betolf / Janjetye Post | Getuygen | De Vader En Moder
Naem Jacobus Geboren De 20 November Gedopt De 19 Februarey 1797

Ouders | Marten Boudese / Martay Corbey | Getuygen | De Vader. Eu Moder
Naem Pettey Geuld Geboren De 1 Jannewary Gedopt De 19 February 1797

Ouders | Isaac Van Sann / Catteljntye Merselus | Getuygen | De Vader Eu / Auantye Van Sann
Naem Leyeu Geboren De 17 Februarey Gedopt De 12 Marth 1797

Ouders | Metjes Everse / yaunetye Post | Getuygen | De Vader en Moder
Naem Leuau Geboren De 25 Fabruarey Gedopt De 12 Merth 1797

Ouders | Jon Berdou / Lenew Breun | Getuygen | De Vader Eu Moder
Naem David Geboren De 19 February Gedopt De 2 Appril 1797

Ouders | Peter Poulese / Janetye Vau Houten | Getuygen | De Vader En Moder
Naem Neltye Geboren De 25 Fabruary Gedopt De 2 Appril 1797

Ouders | David Dey / Sara Nefe | Getuygen | De Vader En Moder
Naem Johaues Geboren De 14 October 1796 Gedopt De 2 Appril 1797

Ouders | David Acerman / Metje Ernost | Getuygen | De Vader En Moder
Naem Ragel Geboren De 6 Mert Gedopt De 2 Appril 1797

Ouders | Johoues Westervelt / Marye Buskerk | Getuygen | De Vader Eu moder
Naem Maretye Geboren De 8 Mert Gedopt De 2 Appril 1797

Ouders | Henderic Van Aule / Abby Ecer | Getuygen | De Vader En Moder
Naem Minochey Geboren De 27 Mert Gedopt de 17 Apprell 1797

Ouders | Geret Vrelaut | Ragel More | Getuygen | De Vader En Moder
Naem Isaac Geboren De 21 September 1796 Gedopt De 17 Apprill 1797

Ouders | Cornelious T. Dooremus | Jaunetye Van Order | Getuygen | De Vader En Moder
Naem Jaunetye Geboren De 11 Mart Gedopt De 17 Apprill 1797

Ouders | Tomis wills | Ragel Van Derbake | Getuygen | Johones Van Derbake En Abby Terhune
Naem Johonis Geboren De 12 Apprill Gedopt De 7 Mey 1797

Ouders | France Van Wincle | Esebele Archebel | Getuygen | De Vader En Moder
Naem Lenew Geboren De 14 March Gedopt De 7 May 1797

Ouders | Abraham Blawvelt | Elesebeth Herring | Getuygen | De Vader En Moder
Naem Abraham Geboren De 13 Apprill Gedopt De 7 May 1797

Ouders | Henderic Dooremus | mawrijte Jocobese | Getuygen | De Vader En Moder
Naem Henderic Geboren De 1 May gedoopt De 1 June 1797

Ouders | Hons Speer | Aultye Recar | Getuygen | Jacob Rjcer Corneljyeu Ricer
Naem Pryntye Geboren De 8 Aprill Gedopt De 5 June 1797

Ouders | Jacob Van Riper | Marretye Vrelant | Getuygen | De Vader En Moder
Naem Gerretye Geboren De 25 Apprill Gedopt de 5 June 1797

Ouders | Jacobes Westervelt | Elesebeth Demorey | Getuygen | David Demorey Annauty Van Saun
Naem Hester Geboren De 3 May Gedopt De 25 June 1795

Ouders | Geljue Acerman | Trynte Manderveal | Getuygen | De Vader En Moder
Naem Leyeu Geboren De 17 November 1796 Gedopt De 25 June 1797

Ouders | Tomes Van Order | Leeu Retou | Getuygen | De Vader En Moder
Naem Sara Geboren De 12 Apprill Gedopt De 16 July 1797

Cuders | Jan Gutchers | Annautye Deter | Getuygen | De Vader En Moder
Naem Hester Geboren De 10 June Gedopt De 16 July 1797

Onders | Jose Cocoru | Solley Vreroxe | Getuygen | Nicolus Cocoru en Peterye
Naem Necolus Geberen De 26 June Gedopt De 16 July 1797

Ouders | Jon Merselns | Jaunetye Van Riper | Getuygen | Jan Perk* En Arreyeuntye Merselus
Naem Arreyanntye Geboren De 2 Ajustes Gedopt De 27 Ajustis 1797

Ouders | Ryneir I Van Geason | Sarey Cint | Getuygen | Isaac Van Geason En Marye Vensen
Naem Affe Geboren De 7 July gedoopt De 27 Aujustes 1797

Ouders | Meselus Van geison | Jennetye Doorenius | Getuygen | De Vader En Moder
Naem Johannes Geboren De 19 Ajustes Gedopt De 17 September 1797

*John Parke.

Ouders | Henderic Hopper Jacemine Quacenbus | Getuygen | Gerrit Hopper En Derece Acerman
Naem Catrenew Geboren De 28 Aujustes Gedopt De 17 September 1797

Ouders | Herculus Becorn Antye Braun | Getuygen | Jacob Braun En Sara yureyanse
Naem Gerret Geboren De 8 Aujustes Gedopt De 17 September 1797

Ouders | Abraham Acerman Elesebeth Cronk | Getuygen | Jon Merselus En Jannetye Van Riper
Naem Jon Geboren De 14 Aujustes Gedopt De 17 September 1797

Ouders | Cornelious Cint Antye Steg | Getuygen | De Vader En Moder
Naem succe* Geboren De 8 September Gedopt De 8 October 1797

Ouders | Tomis Sigler Leneu Speir | Getuygen | De Vader En Moder
Naem Johonnes Geboren De 27 Ajustes Gedopt De 8 October 1797

Ouders | Johonnis R Van Houten sally Van Busse | Getuygen | Abraham Van Riper En Dose Westervelt
Naem Rulif Geboren De 18 September ? Gedopt De 29 October 1797

Ouders | David Brower Sally Pamer | Getuygen | De Vader En Sara Brower
Naem Sara Geboren De 5 October Gedopt De 29 October 1797

Ouders | Teunis Henneon Ragel Acerman | Getuygen | Peter Henneon En Gerteruy Acerman
Naem Elesabeth Geboren De 8 October Gedopt De 19 November 1797

Ouders | David Benson Elesabeth Van Houten | Getuygen | Gerrebraut Van Houten En Jannetye Gerrese
Naem Derick Geboren De 28 October Gedopt De 19 November 1797

Ouders | Abraham Monerse Hester Manderveil | Getuygen | Johones Van Houten En Cantrenew Erl
Naem Elisebeth Geboren De 15 October Gedopt De 19 November 1797

Ouders | David Blar Beiltye Vrelant | Getuygen | De Vader En Moder
Naem Jannetye Geboren De 6 October Gedopt De 19 November 1797

Ouders | Cristufel Brower Lenew Van Houten | Getuygen | De Vader en Antye Van Houten
Naem Deric Geboren De 13 December Gedopt De 25 December 1797

Ouders | Abraham Witten Catrenew Blowvelt | Getuygen | Isaac Blowvelt Gerteren Blauvate
Naem Isaac Geboren De 12 December 1797 Gedopt do 21 Jannewary 1798

Ouders | Henderic Kipp Cotrenew Dooremus | Getuygen | Cornelus Kipp Tyne Demorey
Naem Crestenew Geboren De 10 Jannewary Gedopt De 11 February 1798

Ouders | William Brower Marea helm | Getuygen | Abraham Brower En Marea Alsworth
Naem Marea Geboren De 7 Jannuary Gedopt De 11 Fabruary 1798

*Soeky; i. e., Sukey.

Ouders | yeles Manderveil / Catrenew Roblin | Getuygen | De / Vader En Moder
Naem Hester Geboren De 16 Jannuary Gedopt De 11 Fabruary 1798

Ouders | Isaac Van Geison / Leneu Speir | Getuygen | Peter Duoremo / En Obegel Cuaro
Naem Geret Geboren De 31 October 1797 Gedoopt De 11 Fabruary 1798

Ouders | Peter Seiliff / Salley Ricer | Getuygen | Isaac Ricer / En leneu Smith
Naem Daniel Geboren De 16 Jannuary Gedopt De 11 Fabruary 1798

Ouders | Jon Steg / Antye Blancher | Getuygen | De Vader En / Catrenew Stag
Naem Catrenew Geboren De 8 Jannuary Gedopt De 11 February 1798

Ouders | Jon Westervelt / Antye Van Riper | Getuygen | Cornelious Westervelt / fytye Westervelt
Naem Cornelious Geboren De 30 Janewary Gedopt De 11 Fabruary 1798

Ouders | Johonnes Speer / Abbe Van Busse | Getuygen | Johones Van Houten / Salley Van Busse
Naem fitye Geboren De 20 December 1797 Gedopt De 4 Mart 1798

Ouders | Gerrit Vrelant / Marogretye Van Riper | Getuygen | De Vader / En Maretye Van Riper
Naem Ragel Geboren De 27 Fabruary Gedopt De 4 Mart 1798

Ouders | John Eagerly / hanna Bacon | Getuygen | De / Vader En Moder
Naem Susanne Geboren De 18 Fabruary Gedopt De 25 Mart 1798

Ouders | Gerit Neafe / Eva Van Houten | Getuygen | Cornelious Van Houten / En Mettye Van Houten
Naem Cornelious Geboren De 27 Fabruary Gedopt De 10 Apprill 1798

Ouders | Jores Dooremus / Antye Retan | Getuygen | De Vader / En Moder
Naem Davit Geboren De 5 Fabruary Gedoopt De 10 Apprill 1798

Ouders | Andreus Hopper / Antye Van Vorhase | Getuygen | Peter Hopper / En Antye Dooremus
Naem Antye Geboren De 10 Mart Gedopt De 10 Apprill 1798

Ouders | Helemugh Van Houten / Lenew Van Blarcom | Getuygen | De Vader / En Moder
Naem Annautye Geboren De 1 Aprill Gedopt De 29 Apprill 1798

Ouders | Daniel Benson / Ragel Dooremus | getuygen | De / Vader En Moder
Naem Davit Geboren De 17 Apprill Gedopt De 13 May 1798

Ouders | Rolef Dooremus / Annatye Dooremus | Getuygen | De Vader / En Moder
Naem Henderic Geboren De 16 Apprill Gedopt De 13 May 1798

Ouders | Robert Van Honten / Lenew Van Geason | Getuygen | De Vader En Moder
Naem Antye Geboren De 2 May Gedopt De 27 May 1798

Ouders | Abraham Willis / Catreneu Post | Getuygen | De / Vader En Moder
Naem Abraham Geboren De 26 Apprill Gedopt De 27 May 1798

Ouders | Jon aerl | Getuygen | Jacob BerDan
Annantys Belyn | | En Catrenen Belyn
Naem Jacob   Geboren De 15 May   Gedopt De 10 June 1798

Ouders | Jon Van Blercom | Getuygen | De Vader
Antye yecobuse | | En Moder
Naem Marea   Geboren De 31 May   Gedopt De 1 July 1798

Ouders | Jon hencok | Getuygen | Mert Van Blarcom
Jannetye Van Blercom | | En Antye Van Vegt
Naem Marea   Geboren De 31 May   Gedopt De 1 July 1798

Ouders | Cornelious Westervelt | Getuygen | De Vader En Moder
Polley Roblin | |
Naem Jon   Geboren De 19 June   Gedopt De 1 July 1798

Ouders | Henderic D Hopper | Getuygen | Jecobus Bogert
Hester Van Gelder | | En Corneleyen Hopper
Naem Ragel   Geboren De 26 June   Gedopt De 12 Aujustes 1798

Ouders | Benjemen Delemeter | Getuygen | De
Cleurtye Van Honten | | Vader En Moder
Naem Samnel   Geboren De 15 July   Gedopt De 2 September 1798

Ouders | Willem Van Daun | Getuygen | De
Elesbeth Dooremus | | Vader En Moder
Naem Marea   Geboren De 10 July   Gedopt De 2 September 1798

Ouders | Rulef Van Houten | Getuygen | De
Antye Van Geason | | Vader En Moder
Naem Cornelious   Geboren De 28 Anjustes   Gedopt De 23 September 1798

Ouders | Jon Tise | Getuygen | Jon Cerlough
Catrenen My | | En Elesebeth Stuls
Naem Jon   Geboren De 23 Aujustes   Gedopt De 23 September 1798

Ouders | Jacob Quacenbus | Getuygen | De
Marea Pake | | Vader En Moder
Naem Sara   Geboren De 24 Aujustes   Gedopt De 23 September 1798

Ouders | Jon Van Houter | Getuygen | Benyemen Spear
Marea Brower | | Annautye Brower
Naem Anautye   Geboren De 12 September   Gedopt De 14 October 1798

Ouders | Obe force | Getuygen | Jon Westervelt
Elesebeth Van Houten | | Antye Van Riper
Naem Johonis   Geboren De 5 September   Gedopt De 14 October 1798

Ouders | Bryant Sheys | Getuygen | De
Annautye Duvall | | Vader En Moder
Naem Jacobus Bryant is Geboren De 22 September   Gedopt De 4 November 1798

Ouders | Cornelious Merselus | Getuygen | De Vader
Mariew Post | | En Antye Merselus
Naem Antye   Geboren De 4 October   Gedopt De 4 November 1798

Ouders | Johonnis Brower | Getuygen | De
Marigretye Wite | | Vader En Moder
Naem Marigretye   Geboren De 4 October   Gedopt De 4 November 1798

Ouders | Nicolus Acerson | Getuygen | Jacob Acerson
Marea Orl | | En Wity Bertolf
Naem Jacob   Geboren De 22 September   Gedopt De 4 November 1798

Ouders | Gerit Brower / Leneu Spear | Getuygen | De Vader En Moder
Naem Geret Geboren De 3 October   Gedopt De 25 November 1798

Ouders | Cornelious Van Riper / Maritye G[a]rrese | Getuygen | De Vader En Moder
Naem Jerre Geborer 4 November   Gedopt De 16 December 1798

Ouders | Lowerence Demorest / Maregret Romine | Getuygen | Samuel Van Saun En Marea Buskerk
Naem Samuel Geboren De 21 October   Gedopt De 16 December 1798

Ouders | Isaac Van Saun / Catlinetye Meselus | Getuygen | De Vader En Moder
Naem Arreyeuntye Geboren De 19 November Gedopt De 16 December 1798

Ouders | David Dey / Sara Nefe | Getuygen | De Vader En Moder
Naem David Geboren De 5 September   Gedopt De 16 December 1798

Ouders | Jon yorks / Marea Lyous | Getuygen | De Vader en Moder
Naem Elesebeth Geboren De 18 October   Gedopt De 26 December 1798

Ouders | hons I Post / Fitye Ryker | Getuygen | Rulif Post En Marretye Post
Naem Marritye Geboren De 24 November 1798   Gedopt De 6 Jannewary 1799

Ouders | Johonnis Ryerson / Antye Van Anle | Getuygen | Horremaun Van Blercom En Elesabeht Van Anle
Naem Hessel Geboren De   1798 Gedopt De 6 Jannewarey 1799

Ouders | Derie H Van Houten / Ragel Post | Getuygen | Gerrebrant Van Houten En Jannetye Gerrese
Naem Gerebrant Geboren De 4 December 1798 Gedopt De 27 Jannewary 1799

Ouders | Henderic Dooremus / Marritye Jecobesse | Getuygen | Jon Dooremus En Nense Ryerson
Naem Jon Geboren De 2 December 1798 Gedopt De 27 Jannewary 1799

Ouders | Cresteyaun Shurte / Marregret Demorey | Getuygen | Davit Demorey Eu Hester Brower
Naem Davit Geboren De 6 Jannuarey Gedopt De 27 Jannuarey 1799

Ouders | Barnt Queeenbus / Caty Randseley | Getuygen | De Vader En Moder
Naem Petrus Geboren De 18 December 1798 Gedopt De 27 Jannuarey 1799

Ouders | Davit Speir / Elesabeht youmens | Getuygen | De Vader En Moder
Naom Polly Gboren De 12 October 1798 Gedopt De 17 Fabruary 1799

Ouders | Lowerence Vau Order / Hendericke Billu | Getuygen | De Vader En Moder
Naem Jacob Geboren De 30 Jannewary Gedopt De 17 Fabruarey 1799

Ouders | Merselus Van Geasen | Getuygen | De Vader
Jaunetye Dooremus | | En Moder
Naem Tomes Geboren De 30 Jannuary Gedopt De 10 Mart 1799

Ouder | Peter Tise | Getuygen | Jon Carlough
Catrenen Beuvanhuysen | | En Elesebeht Stuls
Naem Johonnis Geboren De 20 Fabruary Gedopt De 25 Mart 1799

Ouders | Semeon Van Houten | Getuygen | De
Marea Van Blereom | | Vader En Moder
Naem Annantye Geboren De 17 Mert Gedopt De 14 Apprill 1799

Ouders | Hessel Gerrese | Getuygen | De Vader
Sally Ines | | En Moder
Naem Hessel Geboren De 4 Mart Gedopt De 14 Apprill 1799

Ouders | Lukes Van Anle | Getuygen | De Vader En
Antye Van Derhoof | | Tyne Van Anle
Naem Petrus Geboren De 15 Jannuwary Gedopt De 14 Apprill 1799

Ouders | David Dooremus | Getuygen | De Vader
Sally Romer | | En Catrenan Dooremus
Naem Sally Romer Geboren De 28 Jannewary Gedopt De 28 Apprill 1799

Ouders | Isaac Cronk | Getuygen | De
Jannitye Van Houten | | Vader En Moder
Naem Isaac Geboren De 26 Mart Gedopt De 12 May 1799

*Ouders | John Hancock | Getuygen | De
Jenny Van Blareom | | Vader En Moder
Naem Polly Born the 31 May gedoopt de 16 June 1799

Ouders | Johones Jocabese | Getuygen | De
Elesabeth Coenro | | Vader En Moder
Naem Henderic Geboren De 8 May Gedopte De 26 of May 1799

Theunis Dey Born 26th dey of November 1786
God Father John Dey
God Mother Phebe Dey

Ouders | Jon Van Ryper | Getuygen | De Vader
Gerterny Dooremus | | En Antye Dooremus
Naem Antye Geboren De 16 Apprill Gedopt De 26 May 1799

Ouders | Daniel Blowvelt | Getuygen | Peter Stur
Marregret Pervo | | En Welmitey Westervelt
Naem Welmitye Geboren De 23 December 1798 Gedopt De 26 May 1799

Ouders | france Ryerson | Getuygen | De
Jannetye Lambert | | Vader En Moder
Naem Abraham Geboren De 8 May Gedopt De 26 May 1799

Ouders | Peter Olye | Getuygen | De
Elesabeth Mowerse | | Vader En Moder
Naem Albert gebooren De 17 February Gedopt De 7 July 1799

Ouders | David I Hennion | Getuygen | Tunis Hennion
Antye Kipp | | En Catrenew Kipp
Naem Catrenew Geboren De 26 May Gedoopt De 7 July 1799

*Apparently by an oversight, the writer turned over two leaves together, and resumed the record on the third page after making the last entry. On the second page are the three entries here given. The first is crossed off, but it has been thought best to give it here. The third is written in a different hand, in different ink and evidently at a much later date.

11

Ouders | Megeel Dooremus | Getuygen | De Vader
       | Barbarah Zich | | En Sary Dooremus
Naem David   Geboren De 2 June   Gedopt De 7 July 1799

Onders | Petrus Demorest | Getuygen | De
       | Tyne Benson | | Vader En Moder
Naem Abraham   Geboren 11 June   Gedopt De 7 July 1799

Ouders | Jacob Steg | Getuygen | Jon Vreland
       | Marea Andreas | | En Elesebath Van Houten
Naem Deric   Geboren De 9 June   Gedopt De 18 Anjustes 1799

Onders | Jon Berry | Getuygen | De
       | Polly Dey | | Vader En Moder
Naem Jon   Geboren De 3 July   Gedopt De 18 Anjustes 1799

Ouders | Steve Westervelt | Getuygen | De Vader En Moder
       | Marea Acerson | |
Naem Johonnis   Geboren De 22 July   Gedopt De 18 Anjustes 1799

Ouders | Johonis I Gerrise | Getuygen | De
       | Nansey Van Wincle | | Vader En Moder
Naem Simeon   Geboren De 27 June   Gedopt De 18 Anjustes 1799

Ouders | Johonnis H Gerrese | Getuygen | De
       | Marregretye Van Riper | | Vader En Moder
Naem Marregretye   Geboren De 6 September   Gedopt De 29 September 1799

Ouders | Jacob Van Ryper | Getuygen | De
       | Maretye Vrelant | | Vader En Moder
Naem Elesabeth   Geboren De 31 Augestes   Gedopt De 20 October 1799

Ouders | David Dooremus | Getuygen | De Moder
       | Elesabeth Van Houten | |
Naem David   Geboren De 19 September   Gedopt De 20 October 1799

Ouders | Johonnis Bedon | Getuygen | De
       | Lenew Brenn | | Vader En Moder
Naem Marea   Geboren De 23 September   Gedopt De 20 October 1799

Ouders | Henderic Van Blarcom | Getuygen | David Morenns
       | Derrice Acerman | | En Jannetye Acerman
Naem Jannetye   Geboren De 14 October   Gedopt De 10 November 1799

Ouders | Cornelious Cint | Getuygen | De
       | Antye Steg | | Vader En Moder
Naem John   Geboren De 30 September   Gedopt De 10 Novembr 1799

Ouders | Horremonis Van Order | Getuygen | De Vader
       | Sofie Westervelt | | En Vrouwetye Westervelt
Naem Vrouwetye   Geboren De 1 September   Gedopt De 1 December 1799

Ouders | Jacob Agburse | Getuygen | De
       | Jannetye yorks | | Vader En Moder
Naem Cornelious   Geboren De 9 September   Gedopt De 1 December 1799

Ouders | Henre Mac lene | Getuygen | De
       | Sally Speer | | Vader En Moder
Naem Elesabeth   Geboren De 9 September   Gedopt De 1 December 1799

Ouders | Rem underdone / Jese Retan | Getuygen | James Blauvelt / En Antye Clark
Naem elenew   Geboren De 17 November   Gedopt De 22 December 1799

Ouder | Polley Van Houten | Getuygen | Deric Van Houten / Molley Van Ryper
Naem John   Geboren De 25 November   Gedopt De 29 December 1799

Ouders | Jores Dooremus / Antye Retan | Getuygen | De Vader / En Moder
Naem Rulif   Geboren De 7 December 1799   Gedopt de 12 Jannewary 1800

Ouders | yelas Mandervicl / Caty Roblin | Getuygen | De / Vader En Moder
Naem John   Geboren De 22 December 1797   Gedopt De 2 Fabruary 1800

Ouders | Henderic Kipp / Catrenew Dooremus | Getuygen | De Vader En Moder
Naem Henderic   Geboren De 2 February   Gedopt De 23 February 1800

ouders | Aron Jacobese / Agge Van Riper | Getuygen | De / Vader En Moder
Naem Sara   Geboren De 26 Jannewary   Gedopt De 23 February 1800

Ouders | Jores Dooremus / Antye Retan | Getuygen | De / Vader en Moder
Naem Rulif   Geboren De 7 December 1899*

Ouder | Sara Low | Getuygen | Abraham Low / Marregret Spier
Naem Emmetye Marea   Geboren De 14 September 1799   Gedopt De 23 February 1800

Ouders | Robert Post / Ragel Van Derhoof | Getuygen | Jacobus Post / Elesabeth Van Houten
Naem Catrenew   Geboren De 18 Jannewary   Gedopt De 23 Fabruary 1800

Ouders | Mathew Bowden / Martha Curby | Getuygen | De / Vader En Moder
Naem Mathew Bowden   Geboren De 16 September 1799   Gedopt De 23 Fabruarey 1800

Ouders | David Benson / Elesebeth Van Houten | Getuygen | De / Vader En Moder
Naem Molly   Geboren De 24 Fabruary   Gedopt De 16 Mart 1800

Ouders | Bable Van Houten / Rebacce Brower | Getuygen | De Vader / En Lenew Van Houten
Naem Elesebeth   Geboren De 7 Fabruary   Gedopt De 16 Mart 1800

Ouders | Cornelious Van Blercom / Catrenau Van Blercom | Getuygen | Tone Van Blarcom / Elesebeth Van Horn
Naem Jacemine   Geboren De 23 Fabruary   Gedopt De 6 Apprill 1800

Ouders | Jon Merselus / Jannetye Van Rypen | Getuygen | Peter Merselis / Jannetye Van Wincle
Naem Elo   geboren De 30 Mart   gedoopt De 20 Apprill 1800

Ouders | Deric Van Houten / Ragel Post | Getuygen | De / Vader En Moder
Naem Jaunetye   Geboren De 1 Mart   Gedopt De 20 Apprill 1800

*Evidently a clerical error that is still often made at the beginning of a new year. 1799 is meant.

Ouders | Gerebraut Van Houten | Getuygen | Henderic Kipp
Jannetye Gerrese | | En Catrenau Gerrese
Naem Catrenau   Geboren De 31 Mart   Gedopt De 20 Apprill 1800

Ouders | Nicolus Rycer | Getuygen | De
Anneutye Gerrobrantse | | Vader en Moder
Naem Sara   Geboren De 2 February   Gedopt De 20 Apprill 1800

Ouders | Jan Van Iderstine | Getuygen | De
Marea Miller | | Vader en Moder
Naem Catrenau   Geboren D 8 November 1799   Gedopt De 20 Apprill
1800

Ouders | Aderyeuu Coal | Getuygen | Henderic lutkin
Elesabeth lutkin | | Eva Banta
Naem Henderic   Geboren De 5 Mart   Gedopt De 10 May 1800

Ouders | Abraham Van Blarcom | Getuygen | Joh Van Blarcom
Vrouwetye Van Blarcom | | Antye Jecobose
Naem Henderic   Geboren De 31 Mart   Gedopt De 10 May 1800

May den 8—1800
   Jack Jackson Na gedaune belijdenisse Des Geloofs en aengenomen te
   een Lidmaet Der Gemynte Van Totowow*

Ouders | Jores Dooremus | Getuygen | De Vader En Moder
Eva yong | |
Naem Jores   Geboren De 12 Apprill   Gedopt De 25 May 1800

Ouders | Wellem Vandeun | Getuygen | De
Elesebht Dooremus | | Vader En Moder
Naem Marten   Geboren De 20 Apprill   Gedopt De 25 May 1800

Ouders | Harremones Courte | Getuygen | Henderic Courte
Jannetye Speer | | Antye Beuse
Naem Henderic   Geboren De 22 Mart   Gedopt De 25 May 1800

Ouders | Rulif Van Houten | Getuygen | De
Antye Bedau | | Vader En Moder
Naem Jannetye   Geboren De 29 Apprill   Gedopt De 8 June 1800

Ouders | Cornelions Van Houten | Getuygen | De
fytye Van Houten | | Vader En Moder
Naem Aderyaun   Geboren De 14 May   Gedopt De 8 June 1800

Ouders | Abrham Speer | Getuygen | De
Vanderhoof | | Vader En Moder
Naem   Geboren De 5 May   Gedopt De 22 June 1800

Ouders | William youmans | Getuygen | Hons Rycer
Marea Rycer | | En Elesabeth youmans
Naem Elesabeth   Geboren De 27 Apprill   Gedopt De 29 June 1800

Ouders | Teunis Henniou | Getuygen | De Vader
Ragel Acermau | | en Moder
Naem Teunis   Geboren 21 May   Gedopt De 29 June 1800

Ouders | Merselus Van Genson | Getuygen | De Vader
Jannetye Dooremus | | En Moder
Naem Tomes   Geboren De 13 July   Gedopt De 10 Ajustes 1800

*Mei [Bloei-maand] den 8—1800
Jack Jackson Na [hebbende] gedaan belijdenis des Geloofs en [geweest] aangeno-
men te [zijn] een Lidmaat der Gemeente van Totowa.
   Translation—May 8, 1800.
[Baptized] Jack Jackson after [his] having made profession of faith and been re-
ceived a member of the church at Totowa.

Ouders | Daneil Benson | Getuygen | De Vader
| Ragel Dooremus | | Marea Westervelt
Naem Johonnis Geboren De 25 July Gedopt De 10 Aujustes 1800

Ouders | Johonnis Jacobese | Getuygen | De Vader
| Elesabht Cocorn | | En Peterye Cocuro
Naem Nicolus Geboren De 12 July Gedopt De 10 Aujustes 1800

Ouder | David D Demorest | Getuygen | Albert Van Saun
| Annautye Van Saun | | En Januetye Van Houten
Naem Leyeu Geboren De 22 July Gedopt De 10 Aujestes 1800

Ouders | Robert Van Houten | Getuygen | De Vader
| Laneu Van Geason | | En Elesebht Van Geason
Naem Elesabeht Geboren De 24 July Gedopt De 10 Aujnstes 1800

Ouders | Jon Erl | Getuygen | De Vader En
| Aunautye Belyn | | Moder
Naem Annautye Geboren De 21 Aujestes Gedopt De 21 September
1800

Ouders | Cristeyenn Shurt | Getuygen | De
| Marregretye Demoray | | Vader En Moder
Naem Isaac Geboren De 24 Ajustes Gedopt De 21 September 1800

Ouders | Rulif Van Houten | Getuygen | De Vader
| Antye Van Geason | | En Moder
Naem helenau Geboren De 8 September Gedopt De 28 September
1800

Ouders | Gerrebrant Van Houten | Getuygen | De Vader En Moder
| Ragel Maet |
Naem Cornelious Geboren De 15 September Gedopt De 12 October
1800

Ouders | Henderic Dooremus | Getuygen | Henderic Jecobese
| Marretye Jecobese | | Lenew Van Blarcom
Naem Lenew Geboren De 3 September Gedopt De 12 October 1800

*Door Belydenisse aengenemen en Gedopt De 9 October 1800
Jack Slaaf Van Johanness Post
Deyaren Slavin Van Elesabeth Van Houten

Ouders | Semeon Van Houten | Getuygen | Peter Van Houten
| Marea Van Blercom | | En Leyeu Van Riper
Naem Leyeu Geboren De 11 September Gedopt De 12 October 1800

Ouders | David Dey | Getuygen | De
| Salley Neafe | | Vader En Moder
Naem Peter Geboren De 1 July Gedopt De 12 October 1800

Ouders | Cornelious Kipp | Getuygen | Neceuse Kipp
| Tyne Demorest | | En Leyeu Manderviel
Naem Neceuse Geboren De 7 November Gedopt De 14 December
1800

Ouders | John Dooremus | Getuygen | De Vader
| Mareaw Sight | | En Marregretye Westervelt
Naem fiteye Geboren De 11 November Gedopt De 14 December 1800

*Received on profession, and baptised October 9, 1800. Jack, slave of Johannes
Post.
Slave wench [Deern slaaßn] of Elizabeth Van Houten.

Ouders | Cornelious T Dooremus | Getuygen | Horremaun Van Order
Jannetye Van Order | | Sofia Westervelt
    Naem John   Geboren De 19 November   Gedopt De 26 December 1800

Ouders | Jon Parke | Getuygen | De
Arreyaunye Merselus | | Vader En Moder
    Naem Pette   Geboren De 30 September   Gedopt De 4 November 1798

Ouders | John Parke | Getuygen | De
Areyauntye Merselus | | Vader En Moder
    Naem Jenny   Geboren De 27 November 1800   Gedopt De 4 Jannewarey 1801

Ouders | John I Ryerson | Getuygen | De
Marea Bogert | | Vader En Moder
    Naem Anne   Geboren De 14 December 1800   gedoopt De 4 Jannewarey 1801

Ouders | Obe forse | Getuygen | Peter Van Houten
Elesabeht Van Houten | |
    Naem Peter   Geboren De 10 December 1800   Gedopt De 25 Jannewarey 1801

Ouders | Edo Merselus | Getuygen | Peter Merselus En
Lenew Van Houten | | Jannetye Van Wincle
    Naem Peter   Geboren De 19 December 1800   Gedopt De 25 Jannewary 1801

Ouders | Jon Van Blarcom | Getuygen | De Vader
Antye Jecobese | | En Moder
    Naem Henderic   Geboren De 26 Jannewary   Gedopt De 15 Fabruary 1801

Ouders | Isaac Van Saun | Getuygen | Samuel Van Saun
Cattelinetye Merselus | | Marea Buskerk
    Naem Marea   Geboren De 11 Fabruary   Gedopt De 8 Mart 1801

Ouders | Peter tise | Getuygen | De Vader
Catrenew Buvenhausen | | En Moder
    Naem Peter   Geboren De 3 Jannwary   Gedopt De 8 Mart 1801

*P Ouders | Gerit Merselus | Getuygen | De Vader
Lenew Degraw | | En Marea Berre
    Naem Marea   Geboren De 17 Mart   Gedopt De 15 Apprill 1801

Ouders | David Speer | Getuygen | De
Elesebht youmans | | Vader en Moder
    Naem John   Geboren De 4 Jannewary   Gedopt De 12 Apprill 1801

Ouders | Abraham Willis | Getuygen | De Vader
Catrenew Post | | En Moder
    Naem William   Geboren De 26 Jannwary   Gedopt De 12 Apprill 1801

Ouder | Antye Van Houten | Getuygen | Aderyaun Van Houten
| | En Marretye Codmis
    Naem Marregretye Stils   Geboren De 2 Fabruary   Gedoopt De 12 Apprill 1801

Door Belidnese Aengenomen en Gedopt De 7 May 1801
    Sill   Slaven Van Hesel en Henderic Dooremus   Nence Vrie Slavin†

---

*The meaning of this " P" prefixed to "Ouders" which here occurs a few times can only be conjectured. It perhaps indicates that the parents lived at Preakness.

†Received on profession [of faith] and baptized May 7, 1801. Sill [Celia?], female slave of Hessel and Henry Doremus; Nancy, a free [or freed] slave.

Ouders | John H Dooremus | Getuygen | De Vader
Aultye Zebriske | | En Moder
Naem Henderic   Geboren De 4 June   Gedopt De 28 June 1801

P Ouders | Hesel Hennion | Getuygen | De Vader
Catrenew Brower | | En Annantye Brower
Naem David   Geboren De 16 June   Gedopt De 12 July 1801

P Ouders | Cornelious Rulef Van Houten | Getuygen | De Vader En
Marea Vader | | Arreyauntye Veder
Naem Arreyeuntye   Geboren De 31 May   Gedopt De 12 July 1801

Ouders | Peter Merselus | Getuygen | Jan Mercelus
Jannetye Van Winele | | Jannetye Van Riper
Naem Jannetye   Geboren De 26 June   Gedopt De 19 July 1801

Ouders | Jose Cooper | Getuygen | De Vader
Annantye Cronk | | En Moder
Naem anne   Geboren De 21 May   Gedopt De 19 July 1801

Ouders | Robert Post | Getuygen | De
Ragel Vanderhoof | | Vader En Moder
Naem Elisabeth   Geboren De 17 July   Gedopt De 9 Aujustes 1801

Ouders | Johonnis Berdan | Getuygen | De
Lenew Broun | | Vader En Moder
Naem Albert . Geboren De 31 July   Gedopt De 30 Aujustes 1801

Ouders | Marten Van Blarcom | Getuygen | Jon Van Blarcom
Antye Van Vleck | | En Marea Jecobese
Naem John   Geboren De 1 Ajustes   Gedopt De 30 Anjustes 1801

P Ouders | Henry Mac lene | Getuygen | De
Sally Speer | | Vader En Moder
Naem Marregretye   Geboren De 10 July   Gedopt De 13 September 1801

P Ouders | Jores H Dooremus | Getuygen | De
Antye Retan | | Vader en Moder
Naem John   Geboren De 5 September   Gedopt De 27 September 1801

P Ouders | Wilim Van Deun | Getuygen | De
Elesabeht Dooremus | | Vader En Moder
Naem Eva   Geboren De 29 July   Gedopt De 27 September 1801

Ouders | Simon Vauness | Getuygen | Yeles Vauness
Elisabcht Van Geason | | En Hester Vauness
Naem Yeles   Geboren De 24 September   Gedopt De 11 October 1801

Ouders | Gesilert Leke | Getuygen | De
Lenew Brower | | Vader En Moder
Naem Lenew   Geboren De 16 July   Gedopt De 11 October 1801

Ouders | Migel Dooremus | Getuygen | De Vader
Polly Sight | | En Caty Sight
Naem Catrenew   Geboren De 26 Aujustes   Gedopt De 18 October 1801

Ouders | Jase Cocuro | Getuygen | De
Sartye Vrarexe | | Vader en Moder
Naem Henderic   Geboren De 30 Apprill   Gedopt De 1 November 1801

Ouders | Henderic Cocoro | Getuygen | Johonnis Carlough
Elesabht Bogert | | Elesabcht Stines
Naem Johenis   Geboren De 14 September   Gedopt De 1 November 1801

Ouders | Jacob Egberds / Jenny yorks | Getuygen | De Vader en Moder
Naem Beugemen Deboys Geboren De 26 October Gedopt De 22 November 1801

Ouders | Lawrence Van Order / henke Belyu | Getuygen | De Vader en Moder
Naem Lawrence Geboren De 23 November Gedopt De 13 December 1801

Ouders | Isaac Cronk / Jannetye Van Honten | Getuygen | De Vader Eu Moder
Naem Jacob Van Houten Geboren De 16 October 1801 Gedopt De 3 Jannewary 1802

Ouders | Benoue Cinen / Caty low | Getuygen | De Vader En Polley low
Naem Maria Geboren De 1 Jannewary Gedopt De 24 Jannewary 1802

Ouders | Cristeyenn Churt / Marregretye Demorest | Getuygen | Peter Demorest En Hester Demory
Naem Petrus Geboren De 6 Jannewary 1802 Gedopt De 14 Februewary 1802

Ouders | Jacobes Remson / Antye Steg | Getuygen | De Vader En Moder
Naem Johonnis Geboren De 18 Jannewary Gedopt De 14 Fabruary 1802

Ouders | Helmugh Van Houten / Matye Van Geason | Getuygen | De Vader En Moder
Naem Jaunetye Geboren De 14 January Gedopt De 7 Mart 1802

Ouders | Henderic Speer Jun / Marretye Blowvelt | Getuygen | De Vader Eu Moder
Naem Jacob Geboren De 5 Fabruary Gedopt De 7 Mart 1:02

Ouder | Marretye Van Blercom | Getnygen | Mart Van Blarcom Antye Van Veght
Naem Helmugh Van Wincle Geboren De   Fabruary Gedopt De 28 Mart 1802

Ouders | John Van Iderstine / Marea Miller | Getuygen | De Vader En Moder
Naem Marea Geboren De 1 December 1801 Gedopt De 23 May 1802

Ouders | Petrus Demorest / Tyne Benson | Getuygen | De Vader En Moder
Naem Gerit Geboren De 29 Apprill Gedopt De 23 May 1802

Ouders | Jacob Bedan Junr / Antye Van Houten | Getuygen | De Vader En Moder
Naem Caty Geboren De 16 May Gedopt De 6 Juue 1802

Ouders | Semeon Van Honten / Marea Van Blercom | Getnygen | De Vader En Moder
Naem Elesabeth Geboren De 29 Apprill Gedopt De 6 June 1802

Ouders | Abraham F Post / Poley Zebrisker | Getuygen | De Moder
Naem Albert Geboren De 7 September 1801 Gedopt De 25 July 1802

Ouders | David Demorest Jur / Annautye Vau Sauu | Getuygen | De Vader En Moder
Naem David Geboren De 7 Aujustes Gedopt De 5 September 1802

Ouders | Albert Van Saun | Getuygen | De
Jannetye Van Houten | | Vader En Moder
Naem Samuel Geboren De 22 Anjustes Gedopt De 26 September 1802

Ouders | Jan Broun | Getuygen | De
Elesabeht Jones | | Vader En Moder
Naem Ledeya Geboren De 22 Anjustes Gedopt De 26 September 1802

Ouders | Daneal Benson | Getuygen | De Vader
Ragel Dooremus | | En Sarau Dooremus
Naem Jannetye Geboren De 13 September Gedopt De 17 October 1802

Ouders | Gerrebraut Van Houten | Getuygen | De
Ragel Meat | | Vader En Moder
Naem Marea Geboren De 13 September Gedopt De 17 October 1802

Ouders | Henderic H Dooremus | Getuygen | De
Marretye Jacobese | | Vader En Moder
Naem Ahge Geboren De 1 October Gedopt De 17 October 1802

Tom Slave Van Petrus Van Aule Dore Belideness Aungenomen En Gedopt De 17 October 1802

Ouders | Horremaun Van Order | Getuygen | De
feitye Westervelt | | Vader En Moder
Naem Johannes Geboren De 6 October Gedopt De 7 November 1802

Ouders | Abraham Van Blarcom | Getuygen | Antonye Van Blarcom
Vrowetye Van Blarcom | | En Siwen Vrouw*
Naem Andrew Geboren De 5 November Gedopt De 28 November 1802

Ouders | Adreyann Coel | Getuygen | De Vader
Elesebeth Lutkins | | En Moder
Naem John Geboren De 2 October Gedopt De 28 November 1802

Ouders | Willicm Brower | Getuygen | De Vader
Marea Helm | | En Moder
Naem Henderic Geboren De 28 October gedoopt De 28 November 1802

Ouders | Peter Tise | Getuygen | De
Catreneu Bomen | | Vader En Moder
Naem Jacob Geboren De 27 October Gedopt De 28 November 1802

Ouders | france Ryerson | Getuygen | De Vader En Moder Vore Henderic En Henderic Berry En Leau Lambert Vore leau†
Jannetye Lambert |
‡Naem Henderic En leau Twe Linge Geboren De 24 October Gedopt De 28 November 1802

Ouders | John Jacobese | Getuygen | De Vader En Moder
Elesebeth koeuro |
Naem Johannes Geboren De   Gedopt De 28 November 1802

Ouders | Merselus Van geason | Getuygen | De
Jannetye Dooremus | | Vader En Moder
Naem Matye Geboren De 31 October Gedopt De 19 December 1802

Ouders | Gerret Van Riper | Getuygen | De
Jenny Treuter | | Vader En Moder
Naem Jane Geboren De 25 July 1801 Gedopt De 19 December 1802

*Zijn vrouw, his wife.
†The father and mother for Henderic; and Henderic Berry and Leah Lambert for Leah.
‡Names—Henderic and Leah, twins.
12

Ouders | Helmugh Van Geason | Getuygen | De Vader
Salley Van Ostrandar | | En Rachel Post
Naem Antye   Geboren De 22 November 1802   Gedopt De 1 Jannewary
1803

Ouders | Robert Van Houten | Getuygen | De Vader
Lenew Van Geason | | En Marritye Van Geason
Naem Marritye   Geboren De 28 November 1802   Gedopt De 1 Janne-
wry 1803

Ouders | Rulif Van Houten | Getuygen | De
Antye Van Geason | | Vader En Moder
Naem Maritye   Geboren De 5 December 1802   Gedopt De 1 Jannewary
1803

Ouders | John Parke | Getuygen | De
Arreyauntye Merselis | | Vader En Moder
Naem hannah   Geboren De 6 November 1802   Gedopt De 1 Jannewary
1803

Ouders | John Erl | Getuygen | De
Anncautye Bilyu | | Vader En Moder
Naem Ragel   Geboren De 24 December 1802   Gedopt De 16 Jannewary
1803

Ouders | Henderic Van Blarcom | Getuygen | Jack Acerman
Derece Acerman | | En Agge Cadmis
Naem Jacob   Geboren De 20 february   Gedopt De 20 Mart 1803

Ouders | Cornelious Van Blercom | Getuygen | De
Catreneu Van Blarcom | | Vader En Moder
Naem Jacemintye   Geboren De 25 february   Gedopt De 20 Mart 1803

Ouders | Obediah force | Getuygen | De Moder
Elesbeth Van Houten |
Naem William   Geboren de 13 fabruary   Gedopt De 20 Mart 1803

Ouders | William Hunter | Getuygen | De
Elener Carter | | Vader En Moder
Naem phebe   Geboren De 25 December 1802   Gedopt De 20 Mart 1803

Ouders | Bengemen Delemarter | Getuygen | De
Clartye Van Houten | | Vader En Moder
Naem Antye   Geboren De 11 fabruary   Gedopt De 10 Apprill 1803

Ouders | John Berre | Getuygen | De
Polly Dey | | Vader en Moder
Naem Richard Dey   Geboren De 2 Mart   Gedopt De 10 Apprill 1803

Ouders | John I Van Geason | Getuygen | De
Tyne Van Anle | | Vader En Moder
Naem John   Geboren De 5 December 1802   Gedopt De 16 Jannewary
1803

Ouders | Peter Stevens | Getuygen | De Vader
Anne Daves | | En Cestencu Van Sile
Naem Henderic   Geboren De 1 Day November 1795   Gedopt De 21
Apprill 1803

Ouders | yere Van Riper | Getuygen | De Vader
Elesabeth Van Blarcom | | En Marretye Van Riper
Naem Lencu   Geboren De 13 Mart   Gedopt De 23 Apprill 1803

Ouders | Cornelious R Van Houten | Getnygen | De Vader
Sofia Van Houten | | En Antye Van Houten
Naem Rulif Geboren De 2 May Gedopt De 29 May 1803

Ouders | Jose Cocuro | Getuygen | De
Sara frerexe | | Vader en Moder
Naem Conraut Geboren De 23 May Gedopt De 3 July 1803

Ouders | Jacobes Westervelt | Getuygen | De Vader
Elesabeth Demorey | | En Moder
Naem Effe Geboren De 19 June Gedopt De 17 July 1803

Ouders | Abraham Willis | Getuygen | De Vader
Catreneu Post | | En Moder
Naem Ragel Geboren De 30 June Gedopt De 13 Aujustes 1803

ouders | Cornelious Van Horn | Getuygen | De
Sara Wilson | | Vader En Moder
Naem Jeams Geboren De 28 Aujustes Gedopt De 25 September 1803

Ouders | Jacob Gerreson | Getuygen | De Vader
Leya Wesselse | | En Antye Henneon
Naem John Geboren De 27 Aujustes Gedopt De 25 September 1803

Ouders | Henderecus Gutins | Getuygen | De
Sally Van Bussen | | Vader En Moder
Naem Annautye Geboren De 4 September Gedopt De 5 October 1803

Ouders | John R Van Houten | Getuygen | De Vader
Sally Van Bussen | | En Marretye Van Houten
Naem Annautye Geboren De 23 September Gedopt De 16 October 1803

Ouders | Henderic Cocuro | Getuygen | De Vader
Elesabeth Byert | | En Pterye Cocuro
Naem Polly Geboren De 25 September Gedopt De 16 October 1803

Ouders | Gerit Van Riper | Getuygen | De
Jenny Truter | | Vader En Moder
Naem Polly Geboren De 23 September Gedopt De 30 October 1803

Ouders | John merrenus | Getuygen | De
Peggey Guters | | Vader En Moder
Naem Jannetye Geboren De 6 October Gedopt De 6 November 1803

Ouders | John C Van Riper | Getuygen | De
Vrowetye Van Blarcom | | Vader En Moder
Naem Marretye Geboren De 26 Nóvember 1803 Gedopt De 1 Jannewary 1804

Ouders | Henderic Dooremus | Getuygen | De
Marretye Gecobese | | Vader En Moder
Naem Helmeugh Geboren De 13 Jannewary Gedopt De 12 Fabruary 1804

Ouders | Elies Hogens | Getuygen | De Vader
Martha Acerman | | En Jannetye Acerman
Naem yennece Geboren De 20 Jannewary Gedopt De 12 Fabruwary 1804

Ouders | Helmugh Van Houten | Getuygen | De
Matye Van Genson | | Vader En Moder
Naem Diric Geboren De 13 Jannewary Gedopt De 12 Fabruary 1804

Ouders | Joseph Cooper | Getuygen | De
Anneutye Cronk | | Vader En Moder
Naem George Geboren De 7 Jannewary Gedopt De 4 Mart 1804

Ouders | Abraham Van Houten | Getuygen | De Vader En Moder
Gertenau Mowerse

Naem Aderyeun   Geboren De 26 Jannewary   Gedopt De 25 Mart 1804

Ouders | Johannis I Van Geason | Getuygen | De
Tyne Van Aule | | Vader En Moder

Naem Maria   Geboren De 1 Mart   Gedopt De 8 Apprill 1804

Ouders | Aderyaun Cool | Getuygen | De
Elesabeth Lutkins | | Vader En Moder

Naem Jon Westervelt   Geboren De 30 Apprill   Gedopt De 13 May 1804

Ouders | John Post | Getuygen | De
Marretye Vrelant | | Vader En Moder

Naem Caty   Geboren De 19 Fabruary   Gedopt De 13 May 1804

Ouders | Aderyaun Post | Getuygen | Robert Post
Rachel Van Geason | | Ragel Vanderhof

Naem Johonis   Geboren De 14 Apprill   Gedopt De 13 May 1804

Ouders | Johonnis Van Houten | Getuygen | De Vader
Elesabeth Tomson | | En Annentye Van Blarcom

Naem John   Geboren De 19 December 1803   Gedopt De 20 May 1804

Ouders | Cristayaun Churt | Getuygen | De Vader
Marregret Demorey | | En Moder

Naem Catrenau   Geboren De 1 May   Gedopt De 27 May 1804

Ouders | Cristopher Brower | Getuygon | De Vader
Leneu Van Houten | | En Tyne Van Houten

Naem Cattilinen   Geboren De 21 Apprill   Gedopt 17 June 1804

Ouders | Barent Speer | Getuygen | De Vader
Sara Jecobuse | | En libetye Jecobese

Naem Elesabeth   Geboren De 30 May   Gedopt De 8 July 1804

Ouders | Henderic Sturms | Getuygen | De Vader
Elesabeht Meat | | En Moder

Naem Henderic   Geboren De 10 June   Gedopt De 8 July 1804

Ouders | Gerabrant C Gerrebrant | Getuygen | De Vader
ûtye Everson | | En Moder

Naem Cristupher   Geboren De 26 May   Gedopt De 8 July 1804

Ouders | Nicolus Van Blarcom | Getuygen | Nicase V Blarcom
Polly Kipp | | En Jannetye sine Vrow

Naem Nicolus   Geboren De 8 July   Gedopt De 29 July 1804

Ouders | Jacob Berdan Jn | Getuygen | De Vader
Antye Van Houten | | E Polly Van Houten

Naem Richard   Geboren De 27 Anjustes   Gedopt De 9 Setember 1804

Ouders | William Bogert | Getuygen | De
En | | Vader En Moder

Naem Antye   Geboren De 6 September   Gedopt De 30 September 1804

Ouders | David Benson | Getuygen | De Vader
Elesabeth Van Houten | | En Moder

Naem Rebeca   Geboren De 4 September   Gedopt De 30 September 1804

Ouders | David D Demorey | Getuygen | De
Annantye Van Saun | | Vader En Moder

Naem Hester   Geboren De 28 September   Gedopt 21 October 1804

Ouders | John Van Blarcom | Getuygen | De
Antye Jecobese | Vader En Moder
Naem Antye Geboren De 8 November Gedopt De 2 December 1804

Ouders | Edward Erl | Getuygen | De
Marretye Van Blarcom | Vader En Moder
Naem Marten Geboren De 25 November Gedopt De 30 December 1804

Ouders | Johonnes H Gerreson | Getuygen | De
Marregretye Post | Vader En Moder
Naem Marretye Geboren De 5 Jannewary Gedopt De 24 February 1805

Ouders | Merselus Van Geason | Getuygen | De
Jannetye Dooremus | Vader En Moder
Naem Selley Geboren De 2 Jannewarey Gedopt De 17 Mart 1805

Ouders | Peter Demorest | Getuygen | De
Tyne Benson | Vader en Moder
Naem Mareah Geboren De 17 fabruary Gedopt De 17 Mart 1805

Ouders | Robert Post | Getuygen | John Post
Ragel Vanderhoof | En Jenny Vanderhoof
Naem Johonnis Geboren De 19 Fabrewary Gedoopt De 17 Mart 1805

Ouders | Cornelious P Vreland | Getuygen | De
Dautye Van Derhoof | Vader en Moder
Naem Peter Geboren De 7 Jannewary Gedopt De 17 Mart 1805

Ouders | Benyeman Delameter | Getuygen | De
Claurtye Van Houten | Vader En Moder
Naem Gerret Geboren De 9 Fabrearey Gedopt De 7 Apprill 1805

Ouders | Rulif C Van Houten | Getuygen | De Vader
Antye Van Geason | En Moder
Naem Derich Geboren De 16 Mart Gedopt De 7 Apprill 1805

Ouders | Danniel Bensen | Getuygen | De
Ragel Dooremus | Vader En Moder
Naem Gerret Geboren De 9 fabruary Gedopt De 7 Apprill 1805

Ouders | Helmugh Van Wincle | Getuygen | Peter Merselus
Antye Van Houten | Jannetye V Wincle
• Naem Johonnes Geboren De 22 fabruary Gedopt De 7 Apprill 1805

Ouders | Robert Van Houten | Getuygen | De
Lenen Van Geason | Vader en Moder
Naem Johannes Geboren De 8 March Gedopt De 7 Apprill 1805

Ouders | Rem Hunderdonk* | Getuygen | De Vader
Gesie Retan | En Moder
Naem Elenen Geboren De 1 May Gedopt De 26 May 1805

Ouders | Abraham Van Blarcom | Getuygen | Semeon Van Blarcom
Vrowetye Van Blarcom | En Syn Vrow
Naem Abraham Geboren De 3 May Gedopt De 26 May 1805

Ouders | Gerrebrant Van Houten | Getuygen | De Vader
Ragel Meat | En Moder
Naem Henderic Geboren De 6 May Gedopt De 16 June 1805

Ouders | John D Brown | Getuygen | De
Elesebeth Jons | Vader En Moder
Naem Salley Willing Geboren De 25 May gedopt De 30 June 1805

*Onderdonk.

Ouders | John Deeths / Gowdore Vrelant | Getuygen | De Vader En Moder
Naem Nicolus Geboren De 23 June   Gedopt De 21 July 1805

Ouders | Helmugh Van Houten / leneu Van Blarcom | Getuygen | De Vader En Moder
Naem Leneu Geboren De 21 June   Gedopt De 21 July 1805

Ouders | uriah Van Riper / Marretye Blair | Getuygen | De Vader en Moder
Naem Peggy Geboren De 23 June   Gedopt De 21 July 1805

Ouders | Cornelious Van Ryper / Marretye Gerreson | Getuygen | De Vader En Moder
Naem Jacobes Geboren De 21 June   Gedopt De 21 July 1805

Ouders | Benone Cinyen / Caty Law | Getuygen | De Vader En Moder
Naem Jeams Geboren De 3 June   Gedoopt De 21 July 1805

Ouders | Jacob Gerrison / Lea Weselse | Getuygen | Abraham Van Houten En Annautye Weselse
Naem Annautye Geboren De 4 July   Gedopt De 11 Anjestes 1805

Ouders | Cornelians Van Blarcom / Catreneu Van Blercom | Getuygen | Henderic Van Blercom En Anantye Van Blercom
Naem Annautye Geboren De 30 July   Gedopt De 1 September 1805

Ouders | Jacobus Westervelt / Elesabeth Demorey | Getuygen | De Vader En Moder
Naem Johonnes Geboren De 30 July   Gedopt De 1 September 1805

Ouders | Gerret G Van Wagener / Elenau Schooumeer | Getuygen | De Vader En Moder
Naem Gerret Geboren De 15 Anjustes   Gedopt De 22 September 1805

Ouder | Helmugh H Van Houten / Matye Van Geason | Getuygen | De Vader En Moder
Naem Deric Geboren De 9 Anjustes   Gedopt De 22 September 1805

Ouders | Cristeyaun Shurte / Marregretye Demorey | Getuygen | De Vader Eu Moder
Naem Hester Geboren De 22 October   Gedopt De 17 November 1805

Ouder | Jacob Van Wincle / Polley Helms | Getuygen | De Vader Eu Catliuitye Neafea
Naem Peter Geboren De 2 November   Gedopt De 8 December 1805

Ouders | Epka Brown / Ragel Gutchies | Getuygen | De Vader En Moder
Naem John Geboren De 26 Anjestes   Gedopt De 8 December 1805

Ouders | Helmugh Van Geasen / Salley Van Ostrander | Getuygen | De Vader En Marretye V Geasen
Naem Antye Geboren De 22 November   Gedopt De 29 December 1805

Ouders | Henderic H Dooremus / Marretye Jecobse | Getuygen | Henderic Kipp En Elesebeth Kipp
Naem Catreneu Geboren De 6 December 1805   Gedopt De 12 Jaunewary 1806

Ouders | Cornelious Van Horn / Sara Wilson | Getuygen | De Vader En Moder
Naem Ledea Geboren De 26 Janwary   Gedopt De 23 fabruary 1806

Ouders | John Gutyes | Getuygen | Jou Gutyes
Jenny Acerman | | Anantye Gutyes
Vore Annautye En Henderic
Twelingen · Van Blarcom Derrece Van Blercom Vore Jacob
Naem Jacob En Annautye Geboren De 5 Jannewary Gedopt De 23
february 1806*

Ouders | John Jacobese | Getuygen | De Vader En Moder En Antoney
Elesabeth Cocuro | | Jacobese E Anty Jacobese
Twelingen Vore Antoney
Naem Antoney En Peter Geboren De 1 Jannewary Gedopt De 23 fab-
ruarey 1806

Ouders | John Ennaus | Getuygen | De
Marea Steger | | Vader En Moder
Naem Marregretye Geboren De 9 October Gedopt De 23 fabruary 1806

Ouder | Elesabeth Westervelt | Getuygen | Antye Van Riper

Naem Antye Van Riper Geboren De 10 Jannewarey Gedopt De 16
March 1806

Ouders | Edo Van Wincle | Getuygen | Semoen Van Wincle
Jaunetye Vanderhoof | | En Marretye Merselus
Naem Antye Geboren De 27 fabruary Gedopt De 23 March 1806

Ouders | Jerremiah Brower | Getuygen | De Vader
Caty Cool | | En Moder
Naem Henderic Geboren De 25 March Gedopt De 20 Apprill 1806

Ouders | Nicolus Van Blarcom | Getuygen | De Vader
Polley Kipp | | En Caty Van Blarcom
Naem Catreneu Geboren De 28 March Gedopt De 20 Apprill 1806

Ouders | Symen Y Vanness | Getuygen | De
Elisabeth Van Geason | | Vader En Moder
Naem Matye Geboren de 7 Apprill Gedopt De 11 May 1806

Ouders | Horremanus Courter | Getuygen | De
Jaunetye Spear | | Vader En Moder
Naem Lea Geboren De 27 March Gedopt De 11 May 1806

Ouders | Peter Van Aule Jur | Getuygen | John Dooremus
Jenney Dooremus | | Nancey Ryerson
Naem John Geboren De 3 Apprill Gedopt De 11 May 1806

Marregretye Van Sant Geborens De 23 fabruary 1790 Dore Belideness
Angenomen En Gedopt De 25 May 1806

Ouders | Asa Wright | Getuygen | De Vader
Marregretye Vansantt‡ | | En Moder
Naem John Geboren De 5 Jannewary Gedopt De 25 May 1806

Ouders | Charls Blower | Getuygen | De Vader
Ragel Semens | | En Moder
Naem Marea Geboren De 9 May Gedopt De 29 June 1806

Ouders | Gerrebrant Van Houten | Getuygen | De
Jaunetye Gerrese | | Vader En Moder
Naem Catreneu Geboren De 13 June Gedopt De 20 July 1806

---

*Twins—Jacob and Annautye [Annie]. Sponsors—John Gutyes [Goetschius] and
Anautye Gutyes for [the infant] Annautye; and Henderic Van Blarcom and Derrece
Van Blarcom for [the infant] Jacob.
‡Marregretye was but fifteen years, ten months and thirteen days old when she be-
came a mother.

Ouders | Jacob Van Wincle
Elascbeth Vanderhoof | Getuygen | Seannion Van Wincle
En Catterinetye Neafe
Naem Catterine Geboren De 5 October Gedopt De 16 November 1806

Ouders | Johones H Gerreson
Marregriet Post | Getuygen | De
Vader En Moder
Naem Cornelious geboren De 5 October Gedopt De 14 December 1806

Ouders | Henrey Dooremus
Elsabeth Van Geason | Getuygen | De
Vader En Moder
Naem Jenney Geboren De 2 November Gedopt De 21 December 1806

Ouders | Andrus Acerman
Suce Ryer | Getuygen | Jacob Acerman
Ange Codmes
Naem Jacob Geboren De 25 December 1806 Gedopt De 22 January 1807

Ouders | Tomes Codmes
Marregretye Dooremus | Getuygen | Peter Dooremus
Lenew Berrey
Naem Henderic Geboren De 17 December 1806 Gedopt De 25 January 1807

Ouders | Yerreye Van Riper
Elesabeth Van Blercom | Getuygen | De
Vader en Moder
Naem Audrew Geboren De 9 Jannewary Gedopt De 15 fabruary 1807

Ouders | Abraham Willis
Catrennan Post | Getuygen | De
Vader en Moder
Naem Elesabeth Geboren De 12 December 1806 Gedopt De 8 Mart 1807

Ouders | Robert Van Houten
Leneu Van Geason | Getuygen | Henderic dooremus
Marregret Hennion
Naem Marregretiye Geboren De 15 Mart Gedopt De 12 Aprill 1807

Ouders | Micel Ortley
Catrenneu Syn Wife | Getuygen | De Vader En Moder
Naem Elesabeth Geboren De 29 October 1807 Gedopt De 26 Aprill 1807

Ouders | Teren Collivin[?]
Polley Dooremus | Getuygen | Peter Van Aule
En Jenney Dooremus
Naem Marean Geboren De 24 March Gedopt De 26 Aprill 1807

Ouders | William Clerk
Elemer Clerk | Getuygen | De
Vader En Moder
Naem Roseau Geboren De 2 March Gedopt De 26 Aprill 1807

Ouders | Cornelious Van Blarcom
Catreneu Van Blercom | Getuygen | Henderic Van Blercom
En Catreneu Van Blercom
Naem Annautye Geboren De 28 March Gedopt De 3 May 1807

Ouders | John Ray
Elesabehtt Berrey | Getuygen | De Moder
Naem George Merten Geboren De 5 Aprill Gedopt De 3 May 1807

Ouders | Daniel Schoomaker
Elesabeth Post | Getuygen | De
Vader En Moder
Naem Maria Geboren De 19 March Gedopt De 3 May 1807

Ouders | Harrey Godwin
Marretye Merselus | Getuygen | De
Vader En Moder
Naem Abraham Geboren De 2 May Gedopt De 21 June 1807

Ouders | dannel Benson Ragel Dooremus | Getuygen | de Vader En Moder
Naem Cornelus   Geboren De 12 May   Gedopt De 9 July 1807

Ouders | Horremanus Van Orden titye Westervelt | Getuygen | de Vader En Moder
Naem Aultye   Geboren 4 June   Gedopt De 9 July 1807

Ouders | Johones Van Wincle Arreyauntye Merselus | Getuygen | Cornelius Van Wincle En Anantye Van Riper
Naem Johones   Geboren De 20 May   Gedopt De 12 July 1807

Ouders | John Van Blercom Antye Jacobese | Getuygen | De Vader En Moder
Naem Suke   Geboren De 9 June   Gedopt De 12 July 1807

Ouders | Merselus Van Geason Jannetye Dooremus | Getuygen | De Vader En Moder
Naem Cornelious   Geboren De 10 June   Gedopt De 23 Anjestes 1807

Ouders | Cristeyeun Churth Marregretye Demarest | Getuygen | De Vader En Moder
Naem Catreneu   Geboren De 25 July   Gedopt De 23 Anjustes 1807

Ouders | Gerrebrant Van Houten Ragel Ment | Getuygen | De Vader En Moder
Naem Adderyaun   Geboren De 16 July   Gedopt De 23 Anjustes 1807

Ouders | Robert Poust Ragel Vanderhoof | Getuygen | De Vader En Moder
Naem Cornelious   Geboren De 18 July   Gedopt De 12 September 1807

Ouders | Edo Van Wincle Jenny Vanderhoof | Getuygen | De Vader En Moder
Naem Elesabeth   Geboren De 3 September   Gedopt De 4 October 1807

Ouders | David Hemmion Marretye Garrison | Getuygen | De Vader En Moder
Naem Tomes   Geboren De 24 September   Gedopt De 18 October 1807

Ouders | Abraham Van Houten Catrenau Sipp | Getuygen | De Vader En Moder
Naem Gertruy   Geboren De 17 September   Gedopt De 18 October 1807

Ouders | Johonnes I Westervelt Maria Buskerk | Getuygen | De Vader En Moder
Naem Marregrietye   Geboren De 31 July   Gedopt De 8 October 1807

Ouders | John Van Houten Elesabeth thompson | Getuygen | De vader En Moder
Naem Jane Margeret Geboren De 31 Anjustes 1805 En Robert Geboren De 11 March 1807   Gedopt De 22 October 1807

Ouders | Jacob I Gerreson Lea Weselse | Getuygen | Johonnes Gerreson En Gertrone Ryerson
Naem Gerterau   Geboren De 28 September   Gedopt De 25 October 1807

Ouders | Henderic Cocorn Elesabeth Byerth | Getuygen | De Vader En Moder
Naem Nicolus   Geboren De 23 September   Gedopt De 25 October 1807

Ouders | Johnnes Gutyus Jannetye Acerman | Getuygen | De Vader En Moder
Naem Agge   Geboren De 22 November   Gedopt De 20 December 1807

13

Ouders | Cornelious H Dooremus | Getuygen | De Vader
    | Marretye Vralant | | En Moder
Naem Catreneu   Geboren De 4 November   Gedopt De 20 December 1807

Ouders | Daunel F. Lockwood | Getuygen | De
    | Lenan Jerolemon | | Vader En Moder
Naem Mary Van Heuling   Geboren De 27 November 1807   Gedopt De
10 January 1808

Ouders | Tennis Berdan | Getuygen | De Vader
    | Aultye Van Blarcom | | En Moder
Naem David   Geboren De 24 March 1807   Gedopt De 31 January 1808

Ouders | Helmugh Van Houten | Getuygen | De Vader
    | Mattye Van Geason | | En Moder
Naem Johonniss   Geboren De 3 Jannewary   Gedopt De 31 January
1808

Ouders | Johonnes R Van Houten | Getuygen | De
    | Salley Manderviel | | Vader En Moder
Naem Catreneu   Geboren De 29 December 1807   Gedopt De 21 februarey 1808

Ouders | Rulif C Van Houten | Getuygen | De Vader En Moder
    | Antye Van Geasen | |
Naem Derick   Geboren De 20 Januearey   Gedopt De 21 februarey
1808

Onders | Lodewike Smith | Getuygen | Vader En Moder Vore Annantye
    | Caty Dulhagen | | E Harmonness Carlough Maria Tice
Naem Twelinge   Maria en Annntye Geboren De 15 Jannewary   Gedopt De 13 March 1808

Ouders | Abraham A Post | Getuygen | De
    | Elesabeth Westervelt | | Vader En Moder
Naem Jon   Geboren De 7 fabruary   Gedoopt De 13 Martch 1808

Ouders | David D Demarest | Getuygen | Peter Demorest En
    | Annantye Van Saun | | Hester Demorest
Naem Hester   Geboren De 27 Jauewary   Gedopt De 13 March 1808

Ouders | David Merenns | Getuygen | John Merenus En
    | Leneu gerreson | | Pegge Gntyous
Naem John   Geboren De 1 March   Gedopt De 3 Apprrill 1808

Ouders | Semeon Van Houten | Getuygen | De Moder
    | Marea Van Blercom | |
Naem Henderic   Geboren De 11 October 1807   Gedopt De 3 Apprill
1808

Onders | Nicolus Van Blarcom | Getuygen | De
    | Polley Kipp | | Vader En Moder
Naem Isaac   Geboren De 10 Apprill   Gedopt De 8 May 1808

Onders | Robert Paterson | Getuygen | De
    | Marian Keer | | Vader En Moder
Naem John   Geboren De 5 May 1808   Gedopt De 5 June 1808

Ouders | Deric Banta | Getuygen | De
    | Maria Demorey | | Vader En Moder
Naem Petrus   Geboren De 2 May   Gedopt De 5 June 1808

Ouders | Henderic H Doremus | Getuygen | De
Marretye Jecobese | | Vader En Moder
Naem Dann Geboren De 25 Apprill Gedopt De 26 June 1808

Ouders | Apke Breun | Getuygen | De
Ragel Gutches | | Vader En Moder
Naem Hester Geboren De 8 Apprill Gedopt De 25 June 1808

Ouders | Helmugh Van Geason | Getuygen | De
Salley Van Ostrant | | Vader En Moder
Naem Cristupher Geboren De 17 May Gedopt De 25 June 1808

Ouders | William Dooremus | Getuygen | De
Gerterau Jecobese | | Vader En Moder
Naem Tomis Geboren De 3 May Gedopt De 25 June 1808

Ouder | Polley Lane |

Mary Geboren 22 fabruary 1808

Ouders | James H Dooremus | Getuygen | De
Antye Retan | | Vader En Moder
Naem Lyse van Geboren De 7 Juene Gedopt De 17 July 1808

Ouder | John Decths | Getuygen | [De]
Goudare Vrelant | | Vader En [Moder]
Naem Marten Easterly Geboren De 3   Gedopt De 17 July 1[808]

Ouders | Jon Cowenover | Getuygen | De
Nance Jacson | | Vader En Moder
Naem Anneutye Geboren De   Gedopt De 1 Jannewary 1803

Ouder | Jack Jacson | Getuygen | De Vader
Selle sine* Vrow | | En Moder
Naem marea Geboren De 20 Mart Gedopt De 21 Appreall 1803

Ouders | Jon Cowenoven | Getuygen | De Vader
Nance sine Vrow | | En Moder
Naem Nance Geboren De 5 July Gedopt De 13 September 1807

Ouders | Jon Cowenoven | Getuygen | De
Nance sine Vrow | | Vader En Moder
Naem Sam Geboren De 30 September Gedopt De 25 December 1809

Ouders | Jacob Cowenoven | Getuygen | Jon Cawenoven
Angenich suyn Vrow | | En Syne Vrow
Naem Nance Geboren De   Gedopt De 9 Janewary 1814

Jude Sisco Baptised the 29 of August 1824 and made a Profestsion and Became a Member

Brptised Parents John Degrote and his wife Prudence [?] John Cowenoven and Nance his wife John Cowenoven Born on the 22d December 1821 Baptised the 24 of November 1822.

*ziin, his.

APPENDIX.

I.

"A LEST OF SALLIRY FOR DOMINY SCHOONMAKER."

Cornelius Van Winkle	x	x	x	x	x	"	11	"
Abm Van houten	x	x	x	x	x	"	10	"
John Park	x	x	x	x	x	"	4	"
Encress Gould	x	x	x	x	x	"	3	"
Abm Godwin	x	x				"	4	"
Jacob Van houten	x	x	x	x	x	"	2	"
Danel Van horn	x	x	x	x	x	"	2	"
John Ray	x	x	x	x	x	"	2	"
Cornelius Van Blercom	x	x	x	x		"	2	"
James McCordy By Doc								
William Ellison	x	x	x	x		"	2	"
William Brower	x	x	x	x		"	2	"
John flud [Flood]	x	x	x	x	x	"	2	"
Widow king	x	x	x	x	x	"	2	"
hanry Godwin	x	x	x	x	x	"	4	"
Cornelius C Vreeland	x					"	3	"
Danel f Lockwood	x	x	x	x	x	"	2	"
George Doramis	x	x	x	x	x	"	3	"
Banjamin Youmans	x	x	x	x	x	"	2	"
Earon king	x	x	x	x	x	"	2	"
David Spear						"	2	"
Cornelius C Van houten					x	"	3	"
Danel Scoonmaker								
John C Van Ripin	x	x	x	x	x	"	2	6
hanry A Van Blercom	x	x				"	2	"
Abm Van Blercom	x	x				"	2	"
Philip Van Bussen	x					"	2	"
Christopher Brower	x	x	x	x	x	"	2	"
John R Van houten	x					"	2	"
John A Van horn	x					"	2	"
Cornilous J Ryerson'						"	2	"
Thos Wills							4	
Stoffel Van Riper					x		1	
J Shilbur					x		2	
Abrm Stur					x	$ 0	50	
Simeon Van Blarcom					x		37	

[The foregoing "Salliry Lest" is in the writer's possession. It is evidently copied from one or more original subscription lists, and dates probably prior to or about the year 1810. The sign "x" in this case does indeed represent an unknown quantity. This list was probably prepared for the use of the collector, and each time (month or quarter) a subscriber paid, an "x" was marked after his name. The subscriptions were made in shillings and pence, except the last two, which are in Federal money. It is to be hoped that the "Dominy" did not have to depend on this "Salliry Lest" altogether, as it foots up only $12.53.]

II.

"PEW HOLDERS OF THE FIRST REFORMED CHURCH OF TOTOWA."

2	Seats	John D Ryerson	price $ 5		
5	do	David Benson	22		
4	do	Horman Van Norden & Cornelis I Westervelt	17	Each 2 Seats	
5	do	Jacob Van Houten & France Van Winkle	29	do 3 do 2	
4		Richd Van Gieson & Halmah R Van Houter	17	do 2 do 2	
4		Albert Terhune	17		
5		Daniel V Horn	37		
5		Edo P. Mercelis	41		
5		Albert Van Saun	39		
4		Edo Merselis	20		
5		Abrm Ryerson	43	2 Seats	
4		Cornelis C Van Houten	30	2 do	
5		Henry G Doremus	46		
6		Albert Van Houten & Ad Van Houten	21	2 2	
		Rachel Van Houten	22		
4		Ralph Van Houten & Hannah Van Houten	33		
6		Ad R Van Houten	40		
6		John J. Blauvelt & I. I. Stagg	40	do 4 2	
6		Abm R. Van Houten	41		
5		C Van Winkle	45		
5		A Van Blarcom	72	3	
6		Abm Godwin Abm Godwin Jr	32	3 1	
6		P. V. Allen P Van Allen Jr	42	3	
6		G Merselis	30		
6		Albr P Hopper & O P Hopper	30	3	

6	H. Vreeland & A Post	}	33	3 3
6	I. Burhn		33	3
	H Doremus			
6	I. Burhns & I. Sager	}	$16	3 3
6	I. Marinus & D. Marinus	}	11	3 3
5	F. Ryerson & R Degray	}	40	2½ 2½
4	A Parsons		21	
5	H. Van Blarcom		37	
4	D Holsman		20	
5	C Vreeland & G Van Riper	}	40	
5	J. S. Van Winkle & J. J. Berdan	}	35	2½ 2½
4	M. Houghcamp*		19	
5	J. C V. Riper & H. Van Houten	}	32	2½ 2½
5	Andrew Ackerman		26	
4	A & R King		19	½
	J. Flood			2½
5	J. Gutiches J. F. Post	}	25	½
5	C Van Blarcom			
8	J. I. Van Houten			
5	Edo Van Winkle & J Parke	}	27	
5	Jury Van Riper		29	
5	George I Ryerson		35	
5	J. R Berdan Ricd. Berdan	}	30	
5	I. Degrie [? Degray]		48	
5	I. Van Blarcom		51	
5	S. Van Winkle		60	
5	P. Merselis		59	
5	Ad. Van Houten		77	
2½	Abm C Zabriskie		40	
5	G. Van Houten		77	
5	B & J V. Blarcom		71	
5	John J Blauvelt		55	
5	A Van Houten		60	
5	R [?] Zabriskie			

[The foregoing list is from the original in the writer's possession, which was probably prepared between 1820 and 1825.

*Martin Hogencamp.

Compare this with the list of purchasers of pews in 1816, on pages 43–45.]

III.

SUBSCRIPTIONS TOWARDS REBUILDING THE CHURCH.

[When the old Church was destroyed, Dominie Elting and a majority of the Consistory favored building a new Church on the south side of the river, while a majority of the congregation were in favor of rebuilding on the old site. The following is one of the subscription lists for the latter purpose :]

We the subscribers do each of us promise to pay unto Martinus Hogencamp John Joseph Blauvelt Garrabrant Van Houten Abrm R. Vn Houten Adrian R. Van Houten or John Burhans or either of them or their order, the several sums annexed to our respective names, for the purpose of procuring building materials and building a New Church on the scite where the old totoway Church formerly stood with the understanding that the monies thus paid shall be deducted from the purchase money for Pews provided they shall purchase any, when the church shall be finished and pews sold the money so subscribed to be paid in three different equal payments either in money Labour or building materials the first payment to be made on demand, the second payment when the church is raised and the remainder when the same is finished—

Paterson May 14th 1827

G. Van Houten	150	Samuel Vaner*	3
John Jos Blowvelt	100	Peter Van Allen	15
Martinus Hogencamp	50	John R Van Houten	20
Adrian R Van Houten	100	Cornelius G van houten	10
Abm R Van Houten	50	Albert J Zabriskie	50
Wm S Hogencamp	25	Garret Garretson	1.50
Abm Godwin	30	Henery Gacobus	1
A & R. King	50	Thomas Terhune	15
Isaac I Stagg	40	Albert A Terhune	15
Henry Rom	4	Richard F Ryerson	15
John Stagg	30	Tunis Ryerson	20
Ralph Doremus	50		
Abm F Ryerson	15		
Wm Stagg	20		
	714		
John Jacobus	3		

*Query : Van Orden.

Cornelius Van Giesen	5	John A Zabriskie	5
John sneyder	10	Cornelius I Post	2
Saml Quackinbush	1	John Vanness	5
Weart Valintine	10	James Van houten	5
Albert P Hopper	15	Henry A Kiersted	3
Corus G Post	5	Richard Benson	20
Perrigrine Sandford	2	John F Ryerson	15
Nicholas Ackerman	3	Cornelius C Hopper	25

IV.

ANOTHER SUBSCRIPTION TOWARD REBUILDING THE CHURCH.

This list is all in one handwriting, and was doubtless made up from the original subscription lists, in order to keep an account of the payments as made in instalments. It will be observed that some subscribers never paid up in full.

			1	2	3
Garabrant Van Houten	Subscription Church	150	100	50	150
Ralph Doremus	do	150	100	50	150
John Durhaus	do	150	50	50	
Adrian R Van Houten		150	25	110	
Cornelis S. Van Wagoner		50			50
John R Van Houten		50			50
Cornelis I Westervelt		30			30
John Joseph Blauvelt		150		100	
Martinus I Hougheamp*		50		50	50
Francis Cook		5			
Ralph Smith		6			
Albert I Zabriskie		50		50	50
Isaac I Stagg		55			55
John Goutches		20	10	10	20
David Benson		65	25		65
Cornelis P Hopper		75	50		75
Henry Romer		5			
George I Ryerson		50	30		
John R Berdan		77	55	25	77
Richard Berdan		25	12	13	25
Richard Benson		20			20
Thommis Terhune		15	8	7	15
Abraham Van Houten		125	50		
David I Alyea		5			

*Hogencamp
14

	1	2	3
John P Van Allen	10	10	10
Garret G Smith	5		
Peter Van Allen totaway	15	15	15
John Van Allen do	5		
Samuel Burnet* do	5		5
Martin Van Blarcom	2		
John Stagg Jr	30	20	30
Albert A Terhune	15	7	8	15
Garret Garretson totaway			
Perigin Sandfort	5		
Simon Y Van Ness	5		
Cornelis Van Giesen	5		
Giles Van Ness	5		
William I Stagg	20	20	
John Benson	10	10	
Cornelis Post	15	15	15
John Morrow	10	10	10
Susan Ackerman	10		
John Degray	65	65	
Mary Hemion	2		
Albert Terhun	30	30	
John Van Zile	5		
John Berdan	5		
Jacob Berdan	5		
William Brower	5		
John D Ryerson	75		
Jaih† Jackson	5	5	
John Marinus	20	20	
Garret Van Wagoner	10	10	
Peter Sisco	5		
Henry H Post	5		
J. S. friend	5		
George Farrut	5		
John V. A Van Gieson	12		
William Ellison	5	5	
David Marinus	10	10	
B W Van Dervoort	4		
Cornelis G Van Houten	20		
Peter Quckenbush	5		
John Flood	20	20	
James Kearny	4		
John Fine	3		

*Query : Barrett.
†Query : Isaiah.

		1	2	3
Joshua Ackerson		3		
L. White		3		
Aaron King		10	10	10
John N. Ryerson		3		3
Ira Mosher		3		
Henry G. V. Winkle		3		3
Day & Burnet*		2		
Francis Van Blarcom		5		5
E B D Ogden		5		
Nickles† Smith		3		
Andrew Parsons		10		10
James Warren		5		5
Brown King		3		
William Scott		2		
James King		3		
Uriah Garabrant	pd 5	10		
John Willer		5		
Ph. Dickerson		5		
John Ma Intire		2		
Thomas Parker		5		5
Jonathan Hopper		5		
General Abrm Godwin		50		50
John S Forshee		10		10
Peter Archdeken		2		2
Benjm R Romine		10		10
Abrm J Van Winkle		15		15
Halmah Van Houten		5		
Ralph Smith		1		
John Smith		3		3
Antony Van Blarcom		10		10
John Van Ness		10		10
Abrm I Ackerman		3		
Albert P Hopper		25		25
Albert I Hopper		5		5
Daniel Holsman		50		50
Warren Haigh		10		
Henry V. Post		1		1
Henry F Ryerson		10		3.75
Nesbit Talor		5		
Luke Westervelt		25		25
Robert King		15		15
John Lambert		10		10

*Booksellers, and publishers of the Paterson Intelligencer.
†Nicholas.

	1		2	3
Abrm Ackerman Jur	6			
Robert Carrick	60			60
D. K. Allen	20			20
Ezekil Miller	5			5
Henry A Kirste l	5			
James R Post	2			
John A Zabriskie				
Cornelis G Post	5			
Richard Degray	30	10	20	30
Andrew Van Norden	4			
John Snyder	10	7	25	
Richard Van Houten	5			
Isaac S. Miller	5			
Wm. Jacobs	5			
Samul Quekenbush	3			
John W Berry	10			
Stephen S Terhun	3			3
Francis R Post	5			
J. M. Crismon	10			
Jacob Duglas	3			3
John S Van Ness	3			

[$2,599]

V.

The Congregation held several meetings to discuss where the
new church should be built, and on May 20, 1827, at a meeting
of the Consistory held at the house of Judge Gerrebrandt Van
Houten—the old stone house, No. 117 Water street—it was decided to build on a site offered by the Society for Establishing
Useful Manufactures, 130 feet front on Ellison street and about
100 feet deep on Hamilton Square. This led to a vigorous
protest on the part of the dissatisfied members, who appealed
to the Classis of Paramus, which sustained them, and on July
2 the Consistory resolved to abandon the project of building on
the proposed site, and to sell the material already on the
ground, much of the stone of the old church having been cart-
ed thither. Following is the notice of sale, from the original
in the possession of the writer. The paper is about five inches

square, and has in each corner the holes made by the tacks wherewith it was fastened to some convenient fence or door:

Stone & Building Timber

This afternoon between 5 & 6
O'Clock will be sold by auction
All the Stone & Building Timber
lying on the Lot adjoining
the Paterson Bank

By Order of the Trustees of the
1st Reformed Dutch Church Totawa

R Chiswell Auctioneer

5th July 1827

The dissatisfied members withdrew and organized the Second Reformed Church, on October 14, 1827. The First Church secured a site on Main and Ellison streets and Hamilton Square, and erected the church on Main street, where it stood until destroyed by fire in December, 1871.

VI.

PAMPHLETS BY DOMINIE MARINUS.

The first of these pamphlets has the following title:

A | Letter | to the | Independent Reflector | By David Marin Ben Jesse, Pastor at Aquenonka. | New York: | Printed and Sold by Hugh Gaine, at the Printing | Office, opposite the Old Slip, 1753.

Small 4o Pp. 31.

The Letter is dated "Aquenonka, April 5, 1753." The Dominie says: "I who am the least and youngest son of a certain Church in this Province accept your Challenge.—I would rather enter the Lists in Dutch or in Latin, than in the English tongue, being more expert in either of the former, than in the latter." " Whoever believes Christ was the Messiah, and practices the morality He taught, is to all intents and purposes a complete Christian." " To be a Christian is to be a new Creature in Christ Jesus." He makes a long and labored defence of the Clergy, gives a panegyric on William, Duke of Cumberland, and an adjuration to the British. " I am an Englishman born in the Dominions of the best of Kings on earth," he says.

The title of the second pamphlet reads thus :

A | Remark | on the | Disputes and Contentions | in | this Province | By David Marin Ben Jesse, Pastor at | Aquenonka. | Thou shalt not seethe a Kid in his Mother's Milk. Moses. | New-York: Printed by H. Gaine, at the Printing-Office, in Queen-Street, | between the Fly and Meal-Markets, 1755.

Small 4o Pp. 12.

This is an attack on King's (now Columbia) College, because of the apprehended attempt toward a union of Church and State. " The Jersey College (now Princeton) has not succeeded in doing everything." " We intend in time to have a College of our own, for the proper education of our youth." This pamphlet was doubtless intended to have a bearing on the pending troubles between the Cœtus and Conferentie parties. The founding of an American College for the training of young men for the ministry in the Dutch Church in America was a dream of the Cœtus party, which was ultimately realized in the establishment of Queen's (now Rutgers) College at New Brunswick.

INDEX.

INDEX.

15

16

I

J

17

18

www.ingramcontent.com/pod-product-compliance
Lightning Source LLC
Chambersburg PA
CBHW020008030726
47500CB00002B/495